# Praise for Em Petrova's
## *Somethin' Dirty*

"Once you pick this book up it is hard to put down."
~ *Guilty Pleasures Book Reviews*

"This was a story that hooked me fast and kept me interested until the last page. I enjoyed it immensely."
~ *Long and Short Reviews*

"I really enjoyed the sexual tension between Nola and Griffin because it never let up. [...] *Somethin' Dirty* was a fun read."
~ *The Book Pushers*

# Look for these titles by *Em Petrova*

*Now Available:*

*Country Fever*
Hard Ridin'
Lip Lock
Unbroken
Somethin' Dirty

*The Boot Knockers*
Pushin' Buttons
Body Language
Reining Men

# Somethin' Dirty

*Em Petrova*

Samhain Publishing, Ltd.
11821 Mason Montgomery Road, 4B
Cincinnati, OH 45249
www.samhainpublishing.com

Editing by Christa Soule
Cover by Lou Harper

First Samhain Publishing, Ltd. electronic publication: February 2014
First Samhain Publishing, Ltd. print publication: February 2015

# Dedication

"The secret to staying young is to live honestly, eat slowly, and lie about your age."—Lucille Ball

# Chapter One

The piercing wail rose and fell like a fire whistle, gaining in strength by the second. Griffin cracked an eye and came face-to-face with his alarm clock.

Fuck, had he really only just fallen into bed? Twenty-three minutes had passed between the time he'd stripped off his dirty jeans, T-shirt and boots splattered with the filth of pulling a calf, and now his infant daughter was wide awake and ready for six ounces of formula.

"Comin', darlin'." He rolled to his feet and padded in his boxers across the carpet. His little girl's bedroom door was open, and he was assaulted by her cries.

In two strides, he came up against the wooden side of her crib. A glance at her fiery red face and flailing fists tugged his heartstrings.

Scooping her up with one hand, he cradled her against his body. Immediately her cry dropped a notch. She even gave a hiccupping gasp before gearing up with another air raid siren yell.

He flipped her neatly onto his shoulder and patted her back as he made his way to the kitchen. "Now, now, Lyric. You know your daddy isn't gonna starve you. Let's hope Nana made up enough bottles before she left."

He pulled open the fridge, squinting at the glare of light, and saw rows of pre-made bottles lining the bottom shelf like soldiers prepared for war.

"Well, it's a war against your hunger, right?" He dumped the bottle into the warmer and switched it on. Trial and error had taught him the bottle warmer was much faster than the pan of boiling water. Besides, he couldn't overheat and scald his daughter or be forced to endure more of her screams while they waited for the bottle to cool.

He paced the kitchen, bare feet slapping the tile. The little bundle on his shoulder stiffened, ready to produce another wail, but he cupped her and brought her down from his shoulder to look into her face.

Those two dark blue, round eyes blinked up at him with all of the trust in the world. His heart melted.

"Lyric, what am I gonna do with you? If raising you alone is this hard now..." He nuzzled the peachy-soft place between her faint brows and inhaled her baby spice. "You better not give me any trouble as a teenager. Just warnin' ya."

Lyric created a perfect oval with her pink lips, smacking.

"I know you're all ready for this delicious white stuff. Can't wait for you to drink cold cow's milk." He shot a look toward the window. Through the darkness, the shape of the barn rose up. Not even half an hour before, he'd left a brand new calf with its mother after a long night of helping the gangly animal into the world.

"Lots of birthings going on, and I'm not even recovered from yours," Griffin murmured. The bottle warmer switched from a red light to green, indicating it was finished. He plucked out the bottle and shook it. Before he got the nipple to Lyric's mouth, she greedily rooted for it.

She latched on with a ferocious tug, drawing a rumble of laughter from him. He drifted into the open living area of the house he'd built with his own two hands. A long ranch with rooms that rambled one into the next, he'd outfitted it with hard wood, stone and as many creature comforts as he could. His ma had added a few feminine touches—throw pillows and lamps. For his birthday, which was two months after Lyric's, his mother had given him a poster-sized print of Lyric's first day on

Earth.

Now she was four months old and the prize of his life.

He sank to the plush sofa. Every muscle in his shoulders and along his spine protested. Calving season had just begun, and he was already getting little sleep. How was he going to cope with the night feedings in addition to forty-odd head of cattle ready to dump their calves?

Lyric settled in the crook of his arm, and he let his head drop back. Closing his eyes, he drifted until the pull of her mouth on the bottle slowed.

Before he fell asleep, he withdrew the nipple and placed the baby on his shoulder to burp. Little Lyric could take a thumping from her daddy. None of those wimpy, fluttering pats. The thuds jarred her and she let it rip.

"That's my girl," he praised. Sleep descended on him, a blanket thrown over his head. He blinked at the bottle. One ounce left. If he didn't feed it to her, she'd never give him peace.

He stared at her face as she sucked down the rest at a leisurely pace. For months he'd studied his daughter's features, searching for his and her mother's. Would she look like Miranda when she got a little older?

Something inside him hoped not. No doubt he'd made the wrong choice in Miranda. He'd met her at The Hellion, where she waitressed weeknights, trying to put herself through college. As always when he thought of their relationship, he kicked himself for dating a much younger woman.

At forty-two, he knew the man he was and what he wanted from life. He didn't wait around for it to come to him. He went after it.

After he pursued her, Miranda had come willingly into his arms and his bed. For a time, he believed she was the one who would round out his life. The day she'd told him she was pregnant, he'd experienced a leap of joy.

But the pained and terrified look on her face revealed she was less than thrilled. All the diamond rings in the world didn't make her want to have his child. But in the end, money had won out.

If it hadn't been for his friend, Taylor, he never would have found out Miranda was at the abortion clinic until it was too late.

He let his mind drift over those deciding moments, eyes closed and Lyric resting heavily in his arm.


Griffin had hit the parking lot of the abortion clinic in a spray of gravel and dust. His pickup fishtailed, and he quickly stomped on the brake, which sent the back of the truck careening.

He narrowly missed plowing into a shiny luxury SUV— probably the damn abortion doctor's ride.

Jerking the wheel, Griffin landed the truck in the handicap parking spot right in front of the doors. He yanked the emergency brake, and his cowboy boots hit the ground before the vehicle rocked to a complete stop.

The heel of his hand and his shout preceded him into the building. "Where the hell is she? I'm looking for Miranda Hanson." He scoured the waiting room, shocked at the varying ages of the women there. Girls who could barely be out of elementary school to women with the first signs of gray at their temples speckled the room.

*Jesus. She's not here.*

That could only mean one thing. Miranda was already in a room.

Griffin's heart sank to the soles of his boots. Bile formed in the back of his throat. With a roar perched on his lips, he pushed through the door between the waiting room and the office space.

"Sir, you can't be here!" A narrow-shouldered woman tried to block his path, but he pushed her aside with a gentle shove.

"I'm looking for Miranda. You tell me where she is, or I burst into every damn room in this hellish place!"

"No, you can't do that. Sir—"

He swung his gaze left and right. A long hallway ran the length of the building, and about ten sterile white doors lined it. Behind those doors sat women in white paper gowns, awaiting their turn on the abortion table. His stomach hollowed out. Well, it might be all right for some—he wasn't about to tell a woman what she could or couldn't do with her body.

Except when it came to his child.

"Miranda!" he bellowed until his temples throbbed.

The receptionist followed him down the hallway, tugging on the sleeve of his worn denim shirt. "Sir!"

Two doors opened and nurses stuck their heads out. He strode through the office, boot heels thudding. What the nurses saw made them pop back into their rooms.

Griffin grasped a brass door handle and yanked the lever down. "Miranda?" The woman sitting on the table was hollow-eyed, shocked. Not Miranda.

*Please don't let it be too late.*

He opened four more doors before he thundered to the end of the hall. A familiar noise was coming from behind the last door. He swung it open to the sound of pleading.

"Shit, I hear my boyfriend. He doesn't want me to—"

"Damn right I don't, woman!" Griffin slammed the door in the face of the receptionist and stared down Miranda, a nurse and the doctor who was examining her.

"I'm sorry, but you can't be in here," the doctor began.

Griffin closed his hand over the shorter man's shoulder. "Listen, I'm the father of this baby. Surely you have rules about

13

fathers? I get a say in this, so you can make this easy or not. I'm talking to Miranda." With that, he propelled the doctor to the door and shoved him through it. A single glare at the nurse had her scurrying out too. Griffin slammed the door behind them.

Miranda screamed.

In an instant, Griffin was on her. She squealed and writhed like an escaped calf. Gathering both of her hands in one of his, he locked her to the examination table. The scent of sterile things brought the bile back to his throat.

He glared down into her eyes—eyes that had once shone with love for him. But things had changed. They'd fallen apart. He might have loved her back. But not after she'd made the choice to abort their baby.

"You're having this baby, Miranda."

She met his gaze, and a battle of wills ensued. He saw her determination to end this life, and it gutted him.

She twisted violently to break his hold on her, but he pinned her down with a knee on her thighs. The beauty he saw in her was still there, but worn under a mask. He didn't want to know her anymore. Yet he wanted her to give his baby a chance, goddammit.

"Get off me, you—you—"

"Miranda," he breathed, the tears hot on his tongue. He dropped his forehead to hers, holding her completely beneath him. "Please don't do this. I'm begging you."

"I just c-can't have this baby, Griffin. I wish you'd understand! I'm not ready."

No, she probably wasn't. She was twenty years younger than him, and what an idiot he'd been to believe she was in the same place as he was in her life. He was ready for the church wedding and the ever-after. But she wanted to finish college, go on to get her doctorate in psychology. An infant didn't fit into that plan.

"I know you're not ready, Miranda. I fucking know. But I can help. I'll do it all!"

"I couldn't be with you, Griffin. Not now. Our time is past." Tears leaked from the sides of her eyes, which were squeezed shut.

"I know that too. You made it clear you didn't want me in that way anymore. But I am asking you for one thing."

"I can't—"

"Can. Miranda, I'm willing to pay you."

She fell utterly still, her struggle ended with the proposition of money. As the daughter of a single mom, she'd never known abundance, and she was financing herself through college.

She stared up at him.

"Have this baby, and I'll put you through school. I'll pay for everything."

"Books? Food? Housing? Pay off all the past loans?"

"Everything," he vowed, voice as gritty as if he'd gargled glass.

Something dark shifted behind Miranda's eyes, and he moved back, disgusted by how easily she'd been persuaded even as he rejoiced that he might break through her stubbornness.

He leaned away from her, keeping her hands still tucked inside his.

"And all I have to do is have this baby?"

He nodded, sick and thrilled at once. "And sign off it. I'll take full responsibility. But the deal would be just like an adoption. I wouldn't want you entering the child's life five years down the road and confusing her."

Miranda's breath hitched. "Her?"

Griffin pushed off the examination table and backed away. If he didn't get some air, he might throw up. But not pass out. A

15

Wyoming rancher never fainted.

"That's right—her. I had a dream about her, Miranda. Named her Lyric."

Miranda's face crumpled, and she plastered her face with her hands. "Like the song you wrote for me."

"Right now I think I really wrote it for her. So what do you say? Have my baby, and I give you the education you crave. You'll start out fresh without any debt."

She lowered one hand from her face. Tears glistened on each of her fingertips and tracked down her cheeks. Cupping her hand over her belly, she heaved a rough sigh.

"I'm going to get stretch marks."

"Price you gotta pay."

"Will you pay for a tummy tuck too?"

That last remaining coal of warmth he held for Miranda blackened and died. He set his jaw. "My offer stands as is."

She met his gaze, and he saw all of the things she might have been to him. Now he just wanted her body to grow and protect the baby he wanted more.

Finally, she nodded. "Deal."

"Shake on it. I'll have my lawyer draw up papers this afternoon. Until then, I'll accept your word that you won't do..." he waved at the room surrounding them, "...this."

Miranda extended a hand, and he slipped his into it, squeezing her fingers firmly. "I promise."

"Good. Now get dressed, and I'll meet you in the parking lot. I can't bear for my child to be in this place a moment longer."


Lyric straightened her little body like a board, arms rigid.

"Ahh, shit." Neither of them could have been asleep more

than five minutes and now she was gearing up for the colic scream.

He gained his feet and positioned her high on his shoulder as he did a rotation of the living room.

With one hand around the dark, fuzzy head of his daughter, he wondered why he hadn't planned this better. Lyric couldn't have come at a worse time for a rancher. Of course, he hadn't planned it at all.

Lust had claimed his senses, but it wouldn't happen again. One little bundle was enough in his life.

He patted Lyric's back the way his ma did when the child had colic. Thank God Ma came by daily to help out or his ranch would have gone to hell right quick.

Heading down the hall to Lyric's bedroom, he wore the same path back and forth, and finally circled the pretty pink room he'd painted for her. His footsteps grew heavy and his eyelids felt like two sacks of grain.

He'd taken Lyric to the pediatrician two weeks ago, only to find out that some babies had colic and some didn't. Lyric was one of them who did.

"Shh-shh-shh." He shushed into her ear in rhythm to his footfalls.

She bowed her back and screamed louder. Each wail etched itself deep into his heart, flaying his nerves in the meantime.

"Shh-shh-shh."

She gulped for air, filling her lungs to let loose again.

He cupped his hand over her velvety head and nuzzled between her eyes. "Sweet Lyric, it's okay." The song he'd written rose up inside him, bubbling out of his lips without thought.

He hadn't sung it for many months. The words poured out, and he slowed his pace to accompany the beat of the song—a song about a newfound relationship, and how only one lyric was important enough to be sung.

"I love you," he crooned into his daughter's ear.

Her cries mellowed, and her sturdy legs quit churning against his chest. He continued on, singing the same verse. Around and around the room he walked, patting her back, singing his own brand of lullaby, until Lyric went boneless in his hold.

His eyes drooped, and he swayed with fatigue. A glance at the window revealed a slim band of light on the distant horizon. Too soon that sun would rise, and he'd have to slip into his T-shirt, Wranglers and boots and head out for another back-breaking day on the ranch. He couldn't ease off on the workload now—he needed the money more than ever to put Miranda through college.

And the woman had transferred from the community college to an expensive university, damn her.

Griffin stopped walking and sank into the rocking chair with the baby clasped tightly to his chest. He had been rocked in this chair by his mother, and his grandmother had rocked her children in the old hickory chair too.

Lyric didn't have a mother in her life to rock her, but Griffin vowed not to let that weigh into the equation. If he could help it, Lyric would be a happy and well-adjusted child.

"I can't wait to buy you a pair of cowgirl boots," he whispered.

She jerked. Her arms flailed outward at the rasp of his voice, and she issued an eardrum-bursting shriek again.

Griffin put his lips against her ear and started singing to her. All the while he rocked and sang, he wondered how it would have felt to share this responsibility with a good woman.

Nola flipped down the visor and adjusted her sunglasses

against the glare. The last of the spring frost slicked the land, disguising the hills and mountains of Wyoming as marshmallows. Some people called the land pretty, but the sun's position during her commute to work made for a difficult drive.

There were so many other routes into Reedy, but this was the fastest, and she couldn't waste a minute.

She'd gotten out of bed late again.

A glance at the clock on the dash told her that her father wouldn't kill her today for being late to work. If she didn't get behind a slow truck, she'd make it with two minutes to spare.

Filling in by answering phones at his optometry office didn't exactly inspire Nola to get up in the mornings, but it was money in her pocket. If she was going to hit that goal of moving to Nashville to pursue her singing career, she needed dough.

Of course, her daddy had offered her a long-term position in his office, but she couldn't think of anything more annoying than watching people squint at eye charts and giving them opinions on the new frames they'd chosen.

She slowed as she came into Reedy, cursing as she hit the single red light. The little town had a quaint charm to it, but she was ready to get out. Move on with her life. If she didn't leave soon, she'd be in danger of falling victim to some cowboy and living the country life forever.

Her sister, Molly, wanted nothing more than to snag a cowboy. She even worked in the hat and boot shop, hoping it would help her meet Mr. Silver Buckle.

No, that wasn't for Nola. At twenty-five, she was caught in the middle of worlds—too young to settle down and too old to keep dreaming without acting on it. If she wanted this career as a country music singer, she had to jump.

She navigated her economy car off Main Street and into a parking lot where she could pay by the week. Well, Daddy paid.

She climbed out, careful to position her high-heeled boots so she didn't slip on the dew-covered asphalt.

Her father's vehicle was three spaces down, gleaming from a fresh wash. He was maniacal about clean cars—inside and out—and was found in the garage most weekends detailing it.

If he'd already run through the car wash, it meant he'd been at the office for quite a while, probably leafing through the files to ensure she'd done her job correctly.

As she passed his vehicle, she noticed a smudge of dirt on the door—mud thrown by a passing car. She rubbed her thumb over it to remove the dirt, then fished in her purse for a tissue to clean her thumb.

She glanced at her watch. *Annnd, now I'm officially late.*

At least her father would be content with his clean vehicle. She just needed one more bit of ammunition—a special breakfast treat to smooth over the fact she was late.

Sighing, she headed down the sidewalk toward the office. Reedy was just waking up. Most of the shops weren't open yet, which meant Molly was sleeping in. Sisterly irritation wove its way through Nola.

She stopped off in the coffee shop for a Chai tea and a fresh honey bun, which put her seven minutes late. So by the time she reached the office, her father was already trying to talk to the first patient and answer the phone at the same time.

"Sorry, Daddy," she said, rushing forward. She pulled the phone from his hand and gave him both the tea and paper bag. She dropped a kiss to his cheek. "Stopped to get you breakfast." Into the phone, she said in her sweetest voice that dripped of helpfulness, "Good morning, Dr. Brady's office."

Her father stared at her for a long minute, his red brows climbing toward his receding hairline like caterpillars searching for homes. Then with a tilt of his head, he asked the patient to follow him to examination room one.

Looking around the office, despair filled Nola. All she wanted to do was use her voice to entertain people. Since the age of three, she'd vowed to become a country music singer. Now her voice was wasted speaking with insurance companies.

*It's only temporary.*

Nola sank into the office chair, taking information from a new patient over the phone and typing it into the computer. When the call ended, she flopped back, staring at the ceiling, wrists dangling toward the floor.

"I have to get out of this town."

# Chapter Two

"Here comes Nana," Griffin said to Lyric. She flapped her arms and cooed from her pink bouncy seat on the floor.

The whine of his mother's car engine grew louder as she wound up the long drive to his ranch. Six years he'd lived up here, and he adored that driveway. Each corner he rounded, he grew more excited to see the house he'd built, like a kid peeking into store windows at new toys.

He ran his fingers through his hair. Two cups of coffee already hummed in his veins, and he'd gotten five consecutive hours of sleep last night. Lyric's colic seemed to be on the run.

At least he hoped so. The world looked prettier through eyes that weren't so sleep-bleary.

When his mother entered, he had a fresh mug of coffee poured for her, the same way he enjoyed it—black.

A moment passed while she shed boots and coat. He looked up as she appeared around the corner between kitchen and mudroom.

He sucked in a breath. She looked...distraught.

She dropped her teary gaze from his immediately and bent to talk to Lyric. "How's Nana's little baby girl this morning? Your daddy's hair isn't sticking up today. Must mean you slept well."

He stared at his mom's blotchy throat, half covered by her shoulder-length white hair. Alice Turner never flushed unless she'd been crying. The last time he'd seen her cry had been at his grandmother's funeral.

"Did someone die?"

She jerked upright, all the blood draining from her face.

He reached her in one step. Grasping her arm, he steadied her. "Sit down. No, not on the bar stool. It's too high. Here at the table." A table he'd hand-built from white oak. He and Miranda had christened it properly. In fact, it was entirely possible that little Lyric was conceived on it.

His ma slid into the seat and stared straight ahead at the wall.

"What's wrong?" he asked, sitting adjacent to her.

"I had a quick doctor's appointment this morning to go over the results of some tests."

He drew his brows together. "What kind of tests?" His mother was all alone—his dad had taken off in Griffin's early childhood. So Griffin was all she had now.

She carefully wove her fingers together—long and beautifully shaped fingers that reminded him of warm caresses. When she met his gaze, he felt it like a fist in the gut. He hunched forward and grabbed her joined hands.

"Tell me."

It had to be something bad. His happy-go-lucky ma never wore anything but a smile.

"I have a lump, Griffin." Her voice faltered, and his stomach plummeted ten stories. The world made a slow revolution as his shocked mind fought to absorb what she was saying.

She went on. "It's breast cancer. I need a m-mastectomy." She broke down completely.

With a huff of emotion, he leapt out of his chair and enveloped her in his arms, shielding her with his strength the same way he cradled his baby girl.

"Cancer treatments...chemo." She choked. "Losing my hair." The last ended on a wail. She pressed a hand to her head, and flossy white strands clung to her fingers.

He covered her hand. "We'll get through it. I swear we will.

23

You'll be strong and when you're not, I'll be strong for you."

At that, she gave a sniffling laugh. "You're stubborn enough to do just that, Griffin."

He squeezed her tighter. God, how was he going to get through this? He didn't only need her around for his sanity but she was his support system. She couldn't very well take care of Lyric after surgery or make bottles between throwing up from chemotherapy.

His mother sniffed loudly, and his selfish thoughts vanished—smoke in a stiff breeze. This wasn't about him. He'd begged Miranda to have this baby—Lyric was his responsibility. Somehow he'd do it all—run a ranch, raise his daughter and care for his sick mother.

"God, Ma, I'm so sorry." He planted a big kiss on her cheek. She reached up to cradle his jaw.

"I know. Here I sit with a tumor in my breast and I can't help but worry about Lyric."

*Damn, not you too.* He released her and grabbed a box of tissues from a shelf. He sat again as he pushed the box toward his ma. She withdrew two and blew her nose.

Studying her face, he found himself drinking in her features, memorizing the crinkles around her dark brown eyes—eyes like his. What if he never saw her again?

"Stop looking at me like that. I'm not dead yet." Amusement tinged her voice, and he shook his head. She had an uncanny ability to read him.

Lyric cawed, and they both turned to look at her.

"Get my grandbaby out of the seat. I need to hold her."

He got up then unbuckled the side straps holding Lyric in a semi-reclining position. She loved her seat, as she was afforded a good, nosy look around the kitchen.

She cooed and fisted him in the side of the face. He blew a little raspberry on her fingers then passed her to Nana.

While his mother talked to Lyric, he got up and washed out his coffee mug and Lyric's last bottle. Worry dragged at his gut. Could he survive calving season on top of these other obligations?

Damn Miranda for running. What he needed was a mother for his child, but he wasn't about to go hunting for one. Most women his age came with their own baggage—kids, ex-husbands, mortgages. And the younger women were too busy getting doctorates and taking spring breaks to want to take on him, his daughter...and his ill mother.

"Shit," he said under his breath. He turned, leaning against the counter. "You gonna be okay for a bit with her, Ma? I need to see to the animals."

She waved without looking at him, involved in opening and closing her mouth for Lyric's enjoyment.

With mud boots and Carhart jacket on, he went out into the cool spring air. The last of the frost had fled a week ago. The sun's warm fingers slid over his face. Stopping mid-stride, he tilted his face up and let the heat bathe his skin.

The only kiss he'd felt for a long time.

As he tended the few horses he kept and those cows in the barn with calves, he tried to force away the knot of despair in his chest. It was time to man up and hire some help.

But would he hire a ranch hand or a nanny who might assist with the house as well as Lyric? Maybe both.

Having assistance on all fronts would free his time to help his mother by taking her to appointments. Maybe he could move her into the spare room. As soon as the thought struck, he laughed out loud. His independent mother would no sooner move in with him than ride a bucking bull.

He grabbed a pitchfork and dug into the hay, breaking off fresh bits for the cows. Damn, these new hires he was planning would tax his wallet even more. Miranda's demands stretched him thin already. Add health care for a private rancher and his infant daughter and he was nearly poor.

*I'll tighten the belt. Sell the motorcycle. What the hell do I need a motorcycle for, anyway?* He couldn't exactly strap the car seat on the back. And it didn't look as if he'd have a woman to wrap her legs around him anytime soon.

Which led to thoughts of his body's needs. Fuck, he needed to get laid. A real, flesh and blood stress-reducer.

An hour later, muscles warm from exertion and all his animals in the barn tended, he went inside to find his mother and daughter asleep on the couch. Lyric was snuggled belly down, one little fist wrapped around his mother's index finger. It was impossible not to notice the tear tracks on his ma's face.

With a lurch in his stomach, he went in search of the phone book. What he needed to do was place a wanted ad.

Nola shook her hands, trying to flick her anxiety from the ends of her fingertips. The coffeehouse was packed, and she was up next for open mic night. She'd planned this date for a month—sing her heart out to the crowd here, then move on to The Hellion for karaoke and all-you-can-drink Hump Day.

Sure, she'd probably have one too many, but she'd enjoy herself after the rush of performing. And besides, The Hellion provided transportation for all drinkers on these special Wednesdays.

"Ready?" Molly appeared at her side, bouncing on the toes of her red cowgirl boots.

Nola glanced down at her sister's boots. "Take 'em off. Your boots match my outfit better."

Molly's mouth fell open in an O of surprise.

Nola struck with another big-sisterly command. "Now. Hurry. I'm almost up."

"No one is lookin' at your feet," Molly said, hitching up one leg and yanking off her boot. She dropped it and Nola exchanged it with hers.

"If I'm gonna be famous someday, I can't look like a hick. What if someone snaps a photo, and it's sold to the media? I have to look the part." Nola pulled on the other boot and stamped her feet to conform the leather to her shape.

The singer before her—a young guy with an acoustic guitar and a fantastic voice—finished his song on a long, emotional note.

Nola turned to Molly. "How do I look?"

Molly's gaze skimmed her tiny denim skirt and red plaid shirt, knotted just above the waist and exposing a sliver of flesh. She tipped Nola's straw cowgirl hat a bit lower over her eyes. "Perfect. You look mysterious and sexy." She shoved Nola toward the abandoned mic. "Now kick some country ass, sis."

Nola gave her hands one last shake and stepped behind the microphone. Wow. The house really was packed. Every table was filled, and it was standing-room only. She gave a sweeping smile and opened her mouth.

The notes spiraled out, her voice rich and true, just as she'd practiced a hundred times. The recorded music picked up partway through the first verse, as planned. Nola pivoted to Molly and dropped her a nod and a smile of thanks for always being there to back her up.

As she sang, the crowd began to stir, and pretty soon some were on their feet, swaying to the upbeat tempo. This song was a knock-off of a popular ballad. She'd twisted it into a fast song, and it worked pretty well, in her opinion.

She grabbed the microphone from the holder and bent forward, stomping a boot and unleashing her voice's full power on a long note.

The music shut off in perfect timing. And Nola finished the song a cappella—her true strength. Just her and her voice on stage, reaching for the souls of the listeners.

She finished to rousing applause. She fist-punched the air and did a little twirl. Several whistles sounded, and heat infused her face. While she'd dressed to be noticed, it always threw her off-balance.

Male attention wasn't something she wanted or needed at this point in her life, no matter how much she craved it. And whoooeeee, there were a few smokin' hot cowboys in the crowd who could tease her senses.

She gave a final wave and stepped off the small stage. Molly bounced up to her, and they hugged.

"You were great—really strong. All that singin' in the shower paid off."

Nola smacked her and laughed. For her entire life, Molly had made fun of her for singing in the shower. "What can I say? Good acoustics and all that. Let's get outta here. Karaoke's started."

As they moved through the crowd of the coffee shop, Nola accepted praise with a smile, nod and thanks. Once she hit the cooler air, she drew a lungful of breath and calmed a bit.

The performance high lingered though, bubbling just under the surface. A couple of songs at The Hellion, and she'd be flying. This was better than any drug. Hell, it was better than sex.

Maybe not good sex.

Molly drove their grandpa's old pickup with the rusty bed while Nola mulled over her sex life—or lack thereof. Why was she dwelling on it now, of all nights? She'd gone six months without so much as a peck on the cheek from a date. Now she spotted a few pairs of Wranglers and some battered hats, and she was ready for a romp.

"What songs are you going to sing?" Molly asked.

"Umm." She named a few. "That's if that cow Jenna doesn't steal one of them first. You know how she loves to compete with me."

In high school, Jenna had badmouthed her, spread rumors about her and generally did everything in her power to keep Nola from earning the solo performances in choir. Years later, she still tried to steal the spotlight.

Nola waved a hand. "It doesn't matter. She's a good singer, but I'm not competing. My only competition is in Nashville."

Molly turned sad eyes on her. Whenever Nola spoke of leaving Reedy, her sister clammed up and gave her the sad-eye routine.

"Oh c'mon. You know I have to try," Nola said. "Speed up so we can get there and snag a good table."

"Maybe I can get a few twirls on the dance floor with Jamie Poe." Molly's voice grew breathy at the mention of the cowboy she'd been crushing on for months. Jamie Poe was as badass as they came—beautiful physique in ripped jeans, worn boots and an anti-smile that made girls cream themselves. When he leveled that glare at someone...

Nola just hoped it was never her. If anyone got a chance with Jamie Poe, it should be Molly.

The Hellion parking lot was jammed with old trucks and beater cars, looking like submarines in enemy waters. Half of the cars belonged to the designated drivers and the other half to those who planned to take advantage of the all-you-can-drink Hump Day special and then catch a ride home with a sober friend.

One price, as much beer and whiskey as a person could put down without falling over. Most of Reedy would stumble into work bleary-eyed and nauseated the next day. Thank goodness The Hellion only hosted this special once a month.

Nola had no plans to imbibe on that level, but letting her hair down tonight seemed like fun.

*And if I find a cowboy to grind with on the dance floor, even better.*

She shook herself. Where did that come from? Damn, she was intoxicated on the fumes coming from inside The Hellion. Maybe she should stop at one beer, just to be safe. The last thing she needed was a one-night stand. Escaping for Nashville would be harder with a besotted guy tagging behind.

Or worse, what if she became besotted?

She climbed out of the truck and crossed the gravel to the front door of the bar. Determination steeled her spine. No, she was just here to sing and have fun with her sister. No boyfriends, no sex. Just her and a Lady Antebellum song or two.

Inside was hopping. Someone was cranking out Van Halen at the top of his voice, trilling through the octaves as if he were David Lee Roth.

Molly cringed and stepped up to the bar. "Two drafts." She smacked down some bucks, and Nola reached for the wad of cash she'd somehow managed to fit into her skirt. Molly waved her away. "I've got it, sis. You go put your name on the list and choose your songs."

Grinning, Nola swung off through the crowd, pushing against sweaty, excited bodies. The dance floor was wall-to-wall with line dancers and a few couples grinding against each other.

She reached the stage where the karaoke DJ had a binder full of songs. Nola flipped right to her favorites and scribbled her name on the list for three. When scanning the penned names, sure enough, she spotted Jenna's.

Good, let her yodel her way through Taylor Swift.

She whirled to return to Molly, when she lifted her gaze and saw him. Standing against the wall, arms folded, dark eyes hooded as he watched her.

Jesus. Where had this guy come from? Did Reedy even

boast of such amazingly hot men like him? He must be an out-of-towner.

Six-one with messy dark hair that was too long. And damn, he wore a beard with a soul patch under his lip that made her press her thighs together.

His biceps strained the seams of his white and gray western shirt. From here, she saw his jeans conformed to his body, outlining the fact that he was very aware of her.

She shuddered. Confusion gripped her, and before she could do anything remotely stupid like walking up to him and asking for a dance, she spun off into the crowd.

Bodies pressed close, and faces flashed around her. She pressed a palm to her chest, trying to still the manic rate her heart had adopted.

*Be careful. A man like that is a dead weight—a stone tethering you to Reedy.* A hand stopped her, and she looked over to find Molly. Her sister cradled two beers against her tight denim shirt.

"Thanks." Nola took one drink. "Let's get a seat."

Molly laughed, pitching her voice high enough to be heard over the blare. "Where? Maybe that chandelier up there isn't taken." She tilted her head back. "Nope. All clear. Let's climb onto the piano and jump on."

"Okay, we'll stand."

Molly gestured with a nod toward the wall. "Looks like some good standing room over there." Her voice took on an insinuative tone as she obviously spotted Mr. Thigh-Clenchingly-Hot.

"No, not there. We won't be able to see the singers very well."

"You need to see them? Since when?" But Molly followed Nola clear across the room to the opposite wall. An entire dance floor stood between her and that man who, in seconds, had made her forget all dreams of Nashville, and was making her think more and more of how long it had been since she'd had a man's arms around her.

*Or a soul patch rubbing my clit.*

Oh hell no. This wasn't happening. She drank off half of her beer in a few long swallows and stared at the crowd. A lot of people she knew. She waved at friends and nodded to acquaintances, but her mind remained latched to the man against the wall.

She tipped onto the toes of her boots to see him.

A couple shifted on the dance floor, and she caught a perfect view of Mr. Thigh-Clenchingly Hot.

And he was—

"That guy's staring at you. Jesus Lord, Nola." Molly fanned herself. "If a guy was looking at me like that, I'd..."

Nola's mind lost track of Molly's words. Everything around her vanished but those two dark eyes pinning her down.

A movement from Molly snapped her out of it. She looked up in time to see her sister had raised her glass in greeting to Mr. Thigh-Clenchingly Hot.

She wrapped her fingers around Molly's arm. "What the hell are you doing? Don't draw his attention."

"Why not? Have you scored in the past six months? You've gotta be feeling the weight of that stare, sis. Why not invite him onto the dance floor?"

"No, I—" She glanced up to see him pull away from the wall and make his way across the floor. "Oh fuck. Now look what you've done!"

She tried to duck and run into the masses, but Molly hooked a boot around her shin and sent her careening off-balance. Her beer sloshed over the floor, spattering the boots of some dancers.

"So sorry," she mouthed, her voice lost in the stampede of

boots and the cry of appreciation as someone took the microphone for an old Hank Williams song.

Two long, denim-clad legs slid into her vision. She followed the lines up, up, up to the thick chest sporting the white and gray western shirt. And hell, the fabric had a small embroidered flower design next to the pearl buttons.

A man who wore embroidery was very comfortable in his skin. Not a boy. A man.

If she'd had any question about this, she didn't now as she stared into his face. Small lines framed his eyes and lips, and a few threads of silver wove through his beard.

She quivered.

"Wanna dance?" He offered a hand to her, and she gaped at it for two heartbeats.

Before she could think, Molly had divested her of her beer. Then her sister shoved her from behind, and Nola jerked forward. Taking her movement as acceptance, Mr. Thigh-Clenchingly Hot wrapped his fingers around hers and tugged her onto the floor.

Before she could suck in air, she was whipped into his embrace. When she did, she filled her head with his personal musk—man and clean soap. Leather.

He was smiling at her. She returned it, then gave a laugh and dropped her gaze.

He leaned in. "I'm Griffin. And before you ask, this is the first dance I've had in over a year. So don't laugh at my jumbled up feet."

How could she remain aloof to that? Everything about him charmed the pants—or mini-skirt—right off her.

"I'm Nola." She inhaled deeply and didn't catch a hint of beer or whiskey on him. "You're not drinking tonight?"

The corner of his mouth tipped up. "Nah. I'm a designated driver. Love to help out the cause and my ma has the—" He bit

33

off the rest of the sentence with a shake of his head. "My ma taught me to give back to the community."

For several heartbeats, she lost herself in his deep, chocolate gaze. God, were those golden flecks in his eyes? And the creases around each corner enhanced the image that he perpetually squinted into the sun or smiled. Or both.

"Crowded in here," she said a little breathlessly. The bodies hemming her in tighter to Griffin were unwelcome. Weren't they?

Damn, she needed to get away from him, and fast. One more upward quirk of his mouth and she'd be wearing a wedding band and apron.

Would that be so bad? Having someone who loved and cherished her had also been a childhood dream, just as becoming a singer was.

He planted his hand lower on her spine and swayed her toward him until their hips bumped. Lightning shot through her system and pooled between her thighs. The thin scrap of lace covering her pussy did nothing to keep her thighs from becoming wet with moisture.

Griffin grinned at her. "Definitely crowded. Maybe you'd like to step outside for some air?"

Fucking yes. No. She mentally groaned and opened her mouth to reply, though what would burst from her, she had no clue.

"Reedy's own superstar, Nola Brady, up next with some Lady Antebellum. Give her a big hand!"

At the announcement over the speakers, she jerked. Shocked that she'd forgotten all about singing next, or even that the last song had finished and she had simply been locked in Griffin's arms, not dancing at all, she released a hasty breath.

"That's me. Gotta go. Thanks for the dance!"

Before he could grab her back, she threw herself into the

crowd. By the time she made it to the stage, her heart raced. Without a doubt, Griffin would be riveted on her as she sang. Hopefully, she wouldn't choke on her own spit or forget the words.

When the first strains of the song enveloped her and the spotlights heated her face, all of her nervousness vanished. The notes transported her to a joyous place buried deep in her soul.

She was going to do this—get to Nashville and sing for anyone who would listen until the right person heard her.

The way Griffin stared at her as she belted out the song stripped away her boundaries though. He pushed his way to the front of the crowd, so close that if she leaned forward, he could pull her off the small stage into his arms.

A man like that didn't fall into her orbit too often. If she never talked to him again, she'd dwell on it forever.

In a blink, she made up her mind.

She sure as hell was going to have a few more beers tonight, so he could be the one to take her home.

# Chapter Three

What the hell was he thinking? Nola was twenty-five if she was a day. Was her brain even fully formed?

But oh Christ, the sight of her stomping her curvy legs to the beat as she ripped through the notes of that song made him harden painfully. When she flashed him a grin, he focused on her luscious pout and his cock swelled another inch. How, he wasn't sure.

The first two songs she'd sung had blown him away. Reedy's superstar was an understatement. The girl could sing. What was she even doing in small-town Wyoming?

She strutted across the stage on those little red cowgirl boots, the frayed hem of her mini-skirt riding high on her thighs.

He had to get out of here before he lost control. He'd sworn off younger women. Nola was probably a student just like Miranda.

He stared at the dark strawberry blonde waves spilling over her shoulders and reaching for her cleavage, and he knew he was in serious lust. Lust equaled trouble. What could he do anyway? Take her home and halfway through hammer-fucking her over the edge of the bed, Lyric wakes up and screams for a bottle?

He scuffed a hand over his features, trying to wipe away the pounding need that must be evident in his expression. For an hour, he'd shirked his duties as designated driver, allowing others to shuttle people home so he could remain with Nola.

Nola. Her name tasted old-fashioned and brand-new at

once on his tongue. A pretty little thing with tanned legs and a killer voice. What she was doing in Reedy, wasting those talents was beyond him. But he wasn't ready to see her go yet, if that was her plan.

She threw her head back and held a long, throaty note that raised the hair all over his body.

Applause erupted, and he stuck two fingers in his mouth and gave a shrill whistle. When she scanned the crowd and sought him, his balls clenched up tight. That look held more promise than a man of his age and carrying his amount of baggage deserved.

Still, could he pass it up if she offered?

She jumped off the stage for the third time that night, and someone handed her a shot glass brimming full. Some of the amber liquid sloshed down her fingers, and all he could think of was guiding those digits to his mouth and sucking them clean.

Holding his gaze, Nola knocked back the whiskey.

He stepped forward and removed the glass from her hand. Setting it on the edge of the stage, he caught her fingers. She inched close, invading his senses with lush curves and the ripe scent of vanilla and arousal.

Perspiration dotted her throat, and he licked his lips, hungry for a taste.

"You've had too much to drink. I'm taking you home."

"I was hopin' you'd say that." She waved at the redhead who had to be her sister, then pointed at him.

Griffin shot the sister his best nice-guy smile. *No, I'm not a rapist or murderer. I'll see your sister home safe. I just might steal a kiss or more if she'll allow.*

Heart wild in his chest, he wrapped an arm around Nola's waist and guided her out of The Hellion. The brisk night air cut through the heat of his need, and he gulped the coldness into his lungs.

Maybe he shouldn't try anything, just take her home and be honorable.

"My truck's over here." He waved at a well-used truck splattered with mud from the back tires and wished like hell he had something fancy for her.

She walked at his side, as steady as if she hadn't drunk three beers and a whiskey throughout the night. For a little gal like her, that was a lot of alcohol, even spread out over a few hours. She could still sing like crazy even with alcohol in her veins.

By the time he guided her into the truck, he'd made up his mind that he wasn't even going to try to kiss her. But when he got in and she scooted all the way over in her seat, leaning over the console, and threaded a hand into the hair at his nape, all self-control went up in a puff of smoldering hope.

"Where does a guy like you come from? I've never seen you in Reedy before."

"I've lived here all my life." His lips were inches from hers, and her breath washed over him. He studied her hooded eyes and the tips of her lashes, dark with mascara. Stripped of makeup, her lashes would be red-gold.

And the hair between her legs too.

"Hell," he groaned and dropped his mouth to hers.

The first taste punched him in the gut. He snapped his arms around her, hauling her over the console and onto his lap. She clung to him, soft and willing female, her silky thighs draped over his.

He sealed her mouth under his for several seconds then could stand no more. He probed the seam of her lips with his tongue.

She opened to him at once. Her quiet mewl transformed into his croak of need. He trapped her face in his hands and angled her head to sink his tongue deeper into the sweet recesses of her mouth.

Pleasure-pain built in his groin, his erection throbbing against her maddening heat.

He bent her back over his arm until she was pinned to the driver's door, sucking her tongue, nibbling her plump lips.

She wiggled and tugged on his hair, drawing him closer. Her breasts conformed to his chest as if she'd been made for him.

He tore away. Gasping, he stared down at her. She squirmed like a kitten under the gaze of a hawk.

"I'm sorry. I shouldn't..."

She twisted a hank of his hair. "I wanted you to."

"Wanted?" He raised a brow, studying the bead of moisture along her lower lip and wanting more than fucking anything to make it wetter from his kisses. Then he wanted to slip his fingers between her folds and see if she was wet for him in other ways.

His fingers convulsed on her hips. A tiny hole just above the pocket of her skirt allowed him to stroke bare flesh. She shivered, so he did it again. And again.

"Don't stop, Griffin." She pressed her lips to his throat, burning a trail over the beard he probably should have shaved.

"That's the whiskey talkin'." The delicious shocks of want stabbed low. He forced himself to keep from rocking his cock against her.

"I'm totally sober. Besides, I didn't even drink that entire first beer. I spilled it, remember?"

His smile spread, and he turned it against her throat, stamping her with his happiness like a brand. Since the moment he'd set eyes on her, he hadn't been able to look at anyone else. Had it ever been this way for him before?

With Miranda.

It was true that at first, he'd experienced absolute lust for

Em Petrova

Miranda. Could he travel this route again?

Nola squeezed her thigh muscles, cupping his cock perfectly.

Maybe just one night. Then he'd swear off younger women forever. Hell, when he'd signed up to be a driver at The Hellion, he'd never imagined himself in this situation. He was only doing it to get out of the house before his mother's first round of chemo kept him running between ranch and hospital with an infant.

He gently twisted Nola's head to suck on her earlobe. The velvet under his tongue ignited him. With a growl, he cupped her breast. She arched into his touch, a sweet and tender woman to spend all night worshipping.

Except he could only offer her a country road and the bed of his truck.

"Griffin, I'm asking you to take me for a tumble." They lifted their heads and gazed at each other—into each other. She wet her lower lip, and his cock battered his jeans. "It's been so long for me."

"For me too." How long was "so long" to a twenty-five-year-old? Weeks? A month?

No, he couldn't go through with it, no matter how badly he wanted to sink into her heat or how crazy the scent of her excitement made him.

He held her in place. "Listen, baby, I want to. Bad." He let her see the need in him. "But not here, not this way. You've had a few too many, and I don't want to be a regret." He skimmed his hands down her arms to soften the rejection.

A cloud passed over her features, and she dropped her gaze. "You wouldn't be a regret."

"I need to make sure." Gently, he lifted her off his lap and placed her in the passenger's seat. She twisted away from him, arms lashed around her middle as she stared out the side

40

window.

He placed a hand on her knee. "Will you let me take you out sometime?"

She shook her head. "I'm not in the dating game."

Disappointment was ice water trickling over his head, down his shoulders and dousing his desire. So he'd been right in putting on the brakes. He needed a mature woman, not a fling.

"Fair enough." His ragged voice drew her gaze to him again. "But you have to tell me where you live."

She gave him an address, and he put the truck into gear, bumping out of the gravel lot toward the hills where rich daddies kept their little girls safe from guys like him.


After chores and a trip to the outpatient oncology center with his mother, Griffin laid Lyric on a quilt on the floor and positioned a baby gym over her. She happily cooed and batted at a cow jumping over the moon that rattled while he looked over his finances.

His ma would undergo a month of chemotherapy in hopes of shrinking the tumor before surgery. He desperately needed backup. He couldn't exactly haul Lyric into the pasture with him and attempt to care for two hundred head of beef cows.

He tapped his pen against his checkbook and looked at his daughter, who grinned at her toys, mindless of the trouble he was in.

"What am I gonna do with you, little girl?"

The phone pealed, and he removed it from the holder without glancing at the caller ID. "Turner here."

"Uhh...I'm calling about an ad you placed? Looking for a nanny?" The woman's voice faltered.

He sat up straighter. Did he know this caller? The voice sounded familiar. Maybe someone he'd run across in town.

"Yes, I'm looking for a full-time caregiver for my four-month-old daughter in my home up on Needle's Pass."

"I'm interested in the position. What does it pay?"

He gave her a weekly rate, hoping like hell his budget would seriously support it off paper. "What kind of experience do you have?"

"I've babysat for many families since I was thirteen. Recently, I watched my cousins for two weeks while their parents were overseas on vacation. Does that count?"

Since no one else had answered the ad, yes, that counted. In his opinion, if she was flesh and blood and could change a diaper, she was qualified. "Yes, that sounds great. When can you come up and we'll talk?"

"I have some time this morning. I'm helping my dad out at his office in the afternoons only now. At least until I get this job—if I get this job."

"Why don't you come up and we'll discuss the particulars? Then you can meet Lyric."

He detected a smile in her voice. "Lyric?"

"Yes, my daughter." The words to the song he'd written floated through his mind. *Only one lyric important enough to sing for you...* Griffin gave her the address.

"I'll be there in twenty minutes."

He ended the call and stared at the receiver in his hand, wondering about this woman who'd answered his ad. Out of the corner of his eye, he caught a flash of movement. Lyric flapped her arms wildly and rolled onto her belly.

He jumped up and prostrated himself on the floor to stare into her bright blue eyes. "Lyric! You rolled over! You smart girl!"

She stiffened until her body rocked from side to side as if she were a jet ready for take-off. Laughing, he guided her arm up so she could roll without it hindering her, but she just kicked for a minute on her belly. When her face grew red, he rolled her onto her back and kissed her slobbery open mouth.

"Daddy's smart baby. C'mon, doll. Let's get you prettified so you can meet the woman who might be your nanny. Can't have you smelling like that. Not a good impression."

He took Lyric into the bedroom, where he changed her poopy diaper and fed her fat limbs into a fresh one-piece with pink bears on the toes.

By the time he was finished, he had just enough time to glide his fingers through his messy hair and throw a few dishes into the dishwasher. When the knock sounded on the door, he strode forward with Lyric on his shoulder to answer it.

He pulled open the wooden slab and bam. Nearly crumpled at the sight of the red-gold hair.

*Fuck, it's her.* How had she found him? After their almost-encounter that night, he'd thought nothing would come of it.

*Wait. She's here for the nanny job?*

Nola met his gaze, and shock tumbled over her gorgeous features. "I...I must have the wrong house. I'm looking for Turner?"

"That's me. Griffin Turner." Grinning like an idiot, he stepped aside. "Come in."

She did, legs moving woodenly. He shut her inside his house with him, knowing that jerk of wanting low in his core again.

"Umm..."

"I'm looking for a nanny." He flipped Lyric around to face Nola, supporting her around her middle with his forearm. "This is Lyric."

Nola stared at the baby, and he noted the softening around her mouth and eyes. "Ohh. She's as pretty as her name."

*Okay, I'm in love.*

"Come in and sit. We'll talk over coffee. Unless you

43

want...?"

She shook her head. "Coffee is perfect. And for the record, I don't usually drink, you know."

"But you..." he ducked his head, "...remember that night?"

Her face scorched. "Everything about it."

He waved her toward his kitchen table. She sat and removed her coat while he bent and placed Lyric in her bouncy seat. Then he fed the old percolator on the stove with water and fragrant coffee grounds.

Nola laughed. "That's quite domestic for a guy. Actually, all of this is." She looked around at his homey kitchen and daughter.

He met her gaze, dying to cross the floor to her. He crossed his ankles instead, leaning against the counter. "Thank you. I'm a rancher, so good coffee is imperative. It's calving season too, and I'm running full-tilt, supported only by high-test and pure will."

Concern lit her eyes. "So may I ask where Lyric's mom is?"

"Isn't one. I'm raising Lyric alone. Well, with the help of my ma. But she's sick. Breast cancer. It's why I need help."

Nola wrapped her fingers together. "I'm so sorry to hear that. So you need someone during the days?"

*And in my bed at night.*

"That's right." He bobbed his head, trying to fight his awareness of the curve of her breasts in her pale blue sweater or the enticing column of her throat. Too well he recalled her flavor.

"To care for Lyric and what else?"

"Feed her, bathe her, make bottles. Entertain Her Highness." He smiled at his little girl. When he looked back at Nola, she was staring at him in a way that melted his insides.

"Also, some house duties. Baby laundry—I'll do my own. Light cleaning. I don't expect perfection—just a livable place to put my feet up when I come in from the field after an exhausting day."

She nodded. "How old is Lyric again?" She got up and crouched before the baby seat. Lyric watched her with wide eyes. Then she gave a big burp and spit up. Nola froze, and Griffin's alarms went off.

He moved forward. "You can just use the...um, drool bib. She's four months."

Nola glanced at him, a flush settling on her high cheekbones. She gripped the bib and wiped away the spit-up. "You're a sweet baby, aren't you? Even if you're spitting at me." Nola's voice pitched higher, and Lyric flapped her arms. The pink teddy bear feet churned.

"She wants you to pick her up," Griffin said, watching Nola closely. If this was going to work out, she had to be comfortable with Lyric.

"Oh. Okay." Nola looked over her shoulder at him then fiddled with the buckles holding the baby in place. Once the baby was in the striking beauty's arms, Griffin's heart lurched.

*God, yes. I'll curl around you both.*

*No. Bad idea. She's too young, and now she's my employee.*

The baby leaned into her, and Nola lowered her nose to Lyric's head and drank in her scent.

His heart barreled ahead, a runaway horse no one could control. His throat tightened. She was perfect. Fucking perfect.

Nola half-turned to him. "The coffee's ready."

*So am I.*

"What do you think? You want the job? I need someone reliable. It might be for a long spell, at least until my ma gets back on her feet."

The unspoken words hung between them. If she recovers.

Nola nodded, her nose still against Lyric's fuzzy scalp, though a crease of worry lived between her red-gold brows.

"Look, I'm sorry about that night. Between one too many drinks and my singing high, I wasn't thinking straight. I promise I won't let it impact me. I'll take the job. If you want me."

*That's what terrifies me, sweetheart.*


Fuck, a baby. It was the kiss of death to a single woman. Hunky cowboys with puppies Nola could harden her heart against, but this? She was screwed.

*I can always back out of the position.*

Who was she kidding? Excitement battered her insides at the thought of spending all day at Griffin's house. The baby was adorable—and without a ma. It wouldn't take too long to learn how to care for an infant, would it?

Nola bit her lower lip against a rising internal struggle. How easy would it be to slip into this life—to take care of a beautiful, rugged man and his daughter?

No, she was only taking the job to get out of the optometry office. If she didn't, her father would never stop nagging her to take the position permanently. Once she did that, she'd be locked into Reedy forever, typing patient billing information while old ladies peered nearsightedly at her.

Guilt would tether her to her father's office. But this nanny position paid a bit more and she could walk away with only a smidge of regret.

She drove straight to the boot shop to find Molly. Her sister hadn't let up with her questioning about Griffin taking her home. Her romantic sister imagined true love and a happily-ever-after from one ride. Nola was thorns on her sister's roses.

Besides, Griffin had shot down her advances. Actually turned down her offer for sex.

Hell. Could she really work with him?

Maybe she could. Their conversation had been easy today.

He'd given her the tour of his house from one end to the other as well as some of the outbuildings. So if she ever needed him, she'd know where to find him.

The thought sent a stab of excitement to her belly.

Molly was on her knees in front of a cowboy with her "flirt" turned on high as she fitted his new leather boots. Smiling, Nola hung back and watched her sister in action. She practically threw herself at the man, who had to be at least twenty years her senior. Still, Molly didn't care about age—she just wanted to find the man who would complete her soul.

"How do those feel? Don't want anything pinched," Molly said.

Nola shook her head at the insinuative words.

"They're right fine, Ms. Molly. Thank you for your assistance," he drawled, smiling at her.

Molly gained her feet, and Nola beckoned to her.

"What's up, sis? You look as if you just won the lottery."

Damn, she felt as if she'd left Griffin's house with some sort of prize. She schooled her expression.

"No, I got the nanny position."

"That's great, but Daddy's not going to take it well."

"He'll be fine. In fact, once he gets a qualified office assistant, he'll realize what a screw-up I am in that environment."

"Well, he'll miss you buying him Chai teas and honey buns."

Nola laughed. "That's more like it. So, Molly...this guy with the nanny position? He's a single dad."

Molly's eyes popped. "Yeah? And he's gorgeous, isn't he? Tell me he's gorgeous."

"It's Griffin from The Hellion."

Her sister dragged an exaggerated gasp through her lungs. "What?" she squealed. "Oh my God, Nola. It's fate."

Nola shook her head as soon as she saw that word perched on her sister's lips. Since kindergarten, Nola had been telling her it wasn't fate that she and Bobby sat together on the bus. In eighth grade, she'd promised Molly that she and Jordan were not slated for marriage. And on and on.

"No, his ma is sick with cancer, and he needs some help. That's all."

"And the kid? How old?"

Nola tried not to allow her insides to freeze at the thought of being left alone with Lyric. "Four months, a little girl named Lyric."

"Jeezus!" Molly grasped Nola's forearms and shook her. "You're a country singer and he has a kid named Lyric? It's fate, woman! Open your eyes."

Yeah, Nola had mused about that too, but it was coincidence. No matter that if she had her own child, the name would have been a perfect fit.

"When do you start?"

She glanced at her gold watch. "Actually, I need to run. He sent me to the store for diapers and formula. When I get back, I'll take over for a few hours while he tends cattle."

"Lordy, I may faint." Molly fanned herself. "He's a cowboy."

*Ohhh, is he.* Pure male in low-slung jeans and a worn cowboy hat.

Nola ignored the burn between her legs. "Anyway, I won't be home till late tonight. Tell Mom not to keep dinner. I'll probably fix a sandwich at Griffin's."

"You've gotta make chicken marsala for him. It's your best dish."

"It's not a date. I'm taking care of his kid. Okay, you've got a customer. Try not to drape yourself all over him." Nola scooted out the door and back to her car.

She spent an hour trying to find the items on his list. By

the time she paid for the baby supplies, she was rethinking her decision to take the nanny position. Maybe it wouldn't be so bad if she stayed at the optometry office.

Except now that she knew Griffin was in a jam, something deep inside her wanted to reach out and help. All the way back to Needle's Pass, she warred with herself. If she planned to walk away, sooner worked better than later.

It was a bad idea to be around a man she could so easily lose control with. *I'm not the right person for this position.*

When she entered, he was on the phone, the receiver tucked between ear and shoulder and a pissed-off Lyric over his opposite shoulder. Nola's decision to leave him in the lurch vanished. Hurriedly she set the bags down and took the baby.

The bundle squirmed, and Nola panicked. What the hell was she supposed to do with her? She bounced her for a moment, trying to discern what she needed. Fed? Burped?

"Let's start with the basics." She clutched her awkwardly to her chest and peeked between the snaps on the baby's legs. A soggy diaper. With what she hoped was a smile at Griffin, she whisked Lyric down the hall to the changing table.

His voice rose and fell, a low tenor that did things to her insides. She tried to block his voice by talking to Lyric, but he kept invading her senses. A moment later, Lyric was still fussy but clean. Nola's hair tumbled into one eye, and her shirt clung to her damp skin after wrestling two fat legs into a sleeper.

She lifted Lyric and looked up to see Griffin in the doorway, staring at her.

"She's hungry. She's on a four-hour schedule. A minute more than that, and she'll let ya hear it." He grinned lopsidedly, the bracket cutting a path in his cheek. Nola shivered. Too well she recalled the feel of his beard scraping her sensitive skin.

49

And that soul patch...

"Right. I'll handle it if you have work to do."

He gave a short nod. "I do." Still he didn't leave.

Awareness prickled all over her body. Shit, this wasn't what she'd signed up for. She crossed the room, and he stepped aside so she could pass. In the kitchen, she floundered around the space until she found bottle, warmer and burp cloth. He watched her without lifting a hand to find the things for her, which was good because she needed to learn where everything was on her own.

And she didn't want to appear incompetent.

When she sank to the sofa with the baby in her arms, he said, "Looks as if you have everything under control. I'll be outside. Holler if you need me."

A sliver of want did a backstroke down her spine. Without looking up from her task of feeding Lyric, she nodded. "Thanks."

Focusing on the baby, she let her mind wander. What had happened to Lyric's mother? Under what circumstances had Griffin gotten custody of his daughter? And had he loved her mother?

She searched the baby's tiny features for traces of the parents. The fuzz on her head was coming in dark, pointing to her paternal heritage. But perhaps her mother had been dark-haired too.

The child's snub nose and chubby cheeks gave no hint of what she'd look like as an adult. Nola cast a glance around the living room. A field stone fireplace stood cold with ashes, and a thick wooden beam mantel was devoid of photographs. The only picture in the room was a big canvas photo of Lyric as a newborn.

Nola's heart echoed with the emptiness Griffin must feel in his life. No wonder he'd looked at her like that from the doorway. Having a woman in his house, caring for his daughter, probably gave him the feeling of a family.

But not with her. Nope, she was just an employee, stockpiling cash so she could break for Nashville. There, she'd hit all of the local haunts and try to meet with some music executives.

Sated, Lyric drifted into a deep sleep. Nola dreaded even standing up, afraid she'd wake up. Finally, she awkwardly shifted the baby and laid her in the bassinet against the living room wall and covered her with a soft, crocheted blanket. She grinned down at her for a moment. Everything on her was pink, from her sleeper to the pink hearts on her diaper. The blanket and bassinet were both pink, and her bedroom was a pink explosion.

Funny, because a single dad might have chosen more masculine accoutrements for his daughter. One thing was certain—Griffin had a story, and whether Nola liked it or not, curiosity burned in her gut.

She puttered around the living room, cleaning up. Now this she knew how to do.

Then she figured out the washing machine and set it to wash a load of baby clothes. When she turned to leave the small laundry area, a wall of muscle blocked her.

Sucking in a deep breath of surprise was a bad idea. Griffin's musky male spice filled her head.

"Find everything okay?" His voice dipped low, then he cleared his throat. "Need any help?"

She clasped her hands together. "Nope. Got it under control."

He shifted to the side and let her pass. As she moved to the kitchen to continue her chores, her skin prickled. Was he staring at her ass?

Warmth settled low in her belly. As fast as the heat pooled,

Em Petrova

she doused it. The last thing she needed was to feed into her attraction for him. He was dangerous enough with his rugged good looks.

He followed her into the kitchen. While he leaned against the counter, sipping a glass of sweet tea, she opened and closed cupboards to find homes for the clean dishes. Holding a casserole dish, she raised a brow at him.

His heavy stare rooted her to the floor. "Cupboard beside the sink."

"Thanks."

Was he going to hang over her, watching her every move?

Annoyance filtered into her system, followed by the realization that she wanted him to want to be around her.

*Oh no. Time to put on the brakes.*

She spun from the dishwasher but couldn't quite meet his gaze. "Well, that's it for now. Do you need anything before I go?"

"No, everything seems to be in order." He reached out then pulled his hand back and ran it through his hair.

Nodding, she said, "Good. I'll see you tomorrow morning then."

When she moved toward the mudroom, he sidestepped right into her path. Before she gave in to her burning want, she extended her hand to shake his. Professional distance was a must. Sleeping with one's boss was never a good idea. Less so when she didn't want any ropes to bind her to Reedy.

He took her hand, and she curled her toes into the floor at the feel of his work-roughened palm. "Thanks, Nola."

Heart throbbing, she rushed out of the house and shut herself inside her car. As she made her way back down the mountain, she breathed easier. The tension between her and Griffin had to all be in her head. Tomorrow would be easier.

But she had a feeling that keeping a professional distance from the rugged cowboy was going to be like keeping a stallion away from a mare in heat.


Griffin bounced a fussy Lyric on his shoulder and tossed another look out the kitchen window at the driveway. Nola was due any minute, and his internal clock knew it.

Where that woman was concerned, he was far too aware. For the twelfth time since taking her on as nanny, he reminded himself that besides now being on his payroll, Nola was too young. Still, his overactive libido didn't apply an age to desire.

Lyric squawked.

"I know she's late." He glanced at the clock on the range. They hadn't really discussed a time for her to arrive, but he'd assumed she knew ranchers got up early.

He resisted the urge to put Lyric in her bouncy seat and clean up the few breakfast dishes. But if he ignored the mess, he'd have something to talk to Nola about. If he didn't think of a to-do list, he feared what may spurt from his mouth.

Armed with a mental list, he took the baby outside and stared down the driveway. The overcast sky made him eager to get to work before it rained. Where was she?

He let Lyric capture a hank of his hair. After twenty minutes, irritation rolled off him. Nola was living up to his perception of young women.

With his resolve firmly in place again, he went back inside. Seconds later the drone of an engine made his heart leap.

*Dammit, stop that.* He peeked out the window and watched Nola's bare legs emerge from the car.

His cock jerked. Disgusted with his lack of control, he swung from the window and met her at the mudroom door. When she saw his expression, the smile fell from her face.

"Oh no. I'm late, aren't I?"

The uncertain way she nibbled her lip sent Griffin into an

instant state of arousal. But a single look at her fresh, young face helped him clamp off his desires. Wanting this woman was wrong in 500 ways, starting with her age and ending with the fact she was his employee.

"Some dishes in the sink to do. Laundry to fold. And can you change the crib sheets?" He thrust Lyric at her. Awkwardly, she accepted the baby and held her a little apart from her body. "She's been fed and changed. I'll be in the barn."

With that, he stomped outside. Gulping air, he strode faster to put more distance between him and that alluring woman.

But an hour of back-breaking barn work didn't ease the grip she had on him.

Forty more minutes of feeding and watering animals only gave him time to go over ten reasons why she was irresistible.

Twenty more minutes of horseback riding to the top field to check the herd afforded him a better view of his personal goals. No matter how lonely and horny he was, he did not want another Miranda in his life.

His relationship with Nola was strictly professional. He wrote her checks and she cared for his daughter. Simple.

But when he returned to the house for lunch, only to find a covered plate with a sandwich and a few pickles on it, his heart rocked.

He eyed her. "What's this?" He lifted the corner of the plastic wrap covering the plate.

She fidgeted, a faint flush coating her beautiful features. "I figured I was making myself a sandwich anyway and might as well make two."

A kernel of warmth took root in his chest. He pulled off the plastic and lifted the top slice of bread to see a random selection of deli meat and cheese. She didn't know his tastes, but it was the most delicious sandwich he'd ever seen.

And she was the most appealing woman. Replacing the

bread, he met her gaze and smiled. The corners of her mouth twisted up to match his. For an excruciating heartbeat, he battled the need to take her in his arms.

She looked so unsure.

She was fucking perfect.

Dropping her gaze, she said, "I hope the sandwich is okay."

"I can't wait to dig in." He studied her clenched fingers. Was it possible she struggled with the memory of their urgent kisses too?

Nola shot him a weak smile. "Lyric's down for a nap."

"She's right on schedule. She'll wake up ravenous."

"Is there anything you need me to do this afternoon?"

*Yes. Give me a chance.*

*No. Keep sending out those warning vibes. I obviously have some kind of control problem.*

He swept his gaze over the tidy kitchen. It even looked as if she'd mopped. "I can't think of anything. Unless it's folding laundry. Baby laundry is a tedious bitch to fold."

She laughed, a full, sweet sound that reminded him how well she sang. His body reacted with a primal violence. Gut plummeting, cock lengthening, heart squeezing.

To cover the moment, he bit off a huge bite of his sandwich. As he chewed, Nola tilted her head and watched him with an absorption he wanted to cling to.

*She's probably never seen a man make a pig of himself in her presence.*

When he finally swallowed, her gaze drifted up to his. The natural roses in her cheeks deepened in color. "I'll just...check on Lyric."

He gave a short nod. "Sounds good. I'll finish up and get back to work."

As she pivoted, he dug his fingers into his palms to keep from grabbing her back. The luscious view of her ass shook his firm resolve. Lifting the sandwich again, he tried to recall the reasons Nola was all wrong for him.

And then she glanced over her shoulder at him, a wistful expression in her eyes.

*Hell, I'm lost.*

On day four of her being late, Griffin vowed to give her a firm start time. But part of him hoped her erratic schedule would keep him from jumping her. Every minute he waited for her reminded him that she was too young/immature/probably self-centered/off limits.

When he came inside for lunch, no sandwich awaited him. He opened the refrigerator and rifled through a few plastic containers of leftovers. Finding the chicken stir-fry he'd made two nights ago, he popped the lid off and stuck the dish in the microwave.

Nola breezed into the kitchen, her hair in wild disarray. *She looks as if she's been well-loved.*

He shoved the thought away.

Glancing up, she caught his gaze. It held. And held for another long beat of his heart. God, he was so tired of fighting this attraction. Maybe he should let her go and hire some older woman he didn't want to bend over the counter, washer and sofa.

Nola threw him a wave and a tight-lipped smile and went into the laundry room.

The pull was too much. Griffin followed.

Crowding her into the space suddenly felt all right.

She spun to face him, eyes wide, lips parted. "What are you doing?"

Griffin grinned down at her and shook his hair out of his eyes. He hitched his thumb in his front pocket and continued to look at her.

"I've got everything under control." She pressed a palm over her heart.

He pulled away from the wall. One step closer and he invaded her space. Two, and she was pressed against the washer. He braced a hand on the wall cabinet over the appliances and leaned close.

The notes of her perfume sent him reeling. She folded her hands into fists.

His gaze locked on her. For a mind-spinning moment, he fought an inner war.

She ducked under his arm and shot toward the door.

Griffin's heart caved in, and he hung his head for a moment. What the hell was he doing?

# Chapter Four

Griffin scuffed a hand over his face to wipe away the sight of Nola's ass swaying away from him. He felt like a grade-A asshole. She'd been under his employ for under a week, and he was cornering her over a pile of spit-up laundry.

But to be fair, she had looked up at him with those long-lashed blue eyes filled with the same longing he'd seen in The Hellion.

With a shudder he adjusted his dick and followed her to the kitchen. She stood at the sink, rinsing a bottle. The view from the back made him want to bend her over the table. But when she turned, he caught the despair etched on her face.

"Look, I'm sorry about that. I shouldn't have done it. Won't happen again."

She slashed the air with a hand to cut him off. "If you're finished for the day, I'll just be going."

He chewed his lower lip a moment then released it. As far as he knew there weren't any cows in labor, and his ma was home resting. Lyric was down for her late nap, and Griffin probably had an hour of peace ahead of him.

Trouble was, he couldn't think of anything better to fill his time with than kissing Nola.

His cock stirred, and he took a hasty step toward her.

She threw up her hands to ward him off even as she swayed his direction. "I can't get involved with you. I'm going to leave Reedy as soon as I have enough money."

He stared at her. From every angle, wearing countless expressions, she looked as if she'd stepped off the pages of a magazine.

"I'm a singer. I mean, you knew that." She swiped a hand through her strawberry-gold waves. "But my goal is to get to Nashville. Try for something bigger."

A hole blossomed in his gut. He was so right to keep her at arms' length. She needed to get out of Reedy. With beauty and talent like hers she was sure to rise to the top. Some people had it, and she oozed that special something from every delicious pore.

"You have an amazing voice. The world deserves to hear it."

She had goals, just like Miranda. He needed to forget about her being anything but Lyric's caretaker for a few short months. Except she was staring at him that way again—as if she was hungry and only he could hold out the ripe strawberry for her to nibble.

Jeezus. The thought of her lips clamping around something else made his cock bulge to full length. He bit off a groan.

Nola let her gaze wander downward, taking in his arousal. Her blatant perusal turned him on like nothing else. He clenched his hands into fists to keep from grabbing her, throwing her over his shoulder and stomping to his bedroom.

Her gaze traveled up his body, scorching a path that ended on his face. He returned her stare, unapologetic for his state.

Something slipped in her gaze—permission. Welcome.

He took two strides and caught her in his arms. "Griffin," she squeaked a moment before he crushed his mouth to hers.

Lust tingled down his spine as he plunged his tongue between her sweet lips. She melted in his embrace, molding her soft breasts to his chest. He gripped her ass and dragged her against his erection.

Each velvety pass of her tongue tore at his control. He cupped the back of her head and dived deeper. Hell, he never wanted to surface.

She was just as wild. Her short nails dug into his back, and she opened wide to his questing tongue. She tasted spicy like cinnamon or freshly chewed grass.

Tearing away, he pressed gentler kisses to the corner of her lips, her delicate jaw, around her throat to her ear. Her breath came in pants. When he palmed her breast, she gave a quiet cry.

*That's it.* He lifted her off her feet. She wrapped her thighs around his waist and found his lips again as he set her on the counter. She wore denim shorts, a tank top and a denim vest he couldn't wait to peel off.

Dark pressure tightened his groin, and his hips moved on their own. He ground his cock into the V of her legs. The scent of her arousal hit him, and he growled.

He glided a hand under her shirt, over the taut belly he longed to lick, and up to her rounded breast. When the weight filled his hand, he stole a peek at her face.

Want was a song scrawled over her beautiful features. *And I'm going to make you sing it. Over and over again.*

He discarded the vest, lifted her top and pulled her bra fabric until the creamy mound of flesh popped free.

Hell, her nipple was dark and beaded.

With a rumble of need, he trapped it between his lips. Rolling and swirling it until she writhed. She tugged his hair, raising goose bumps all over him. When had that ever happened?

He sucked her bud into his mouth and laved it with his tongue, wanting more, more, more.

"Griffin…"

"Baby, I wanted to do this that night after you bewitched me with your voice. And for the past four days. I can't keep my hands off you anymore."

She stopped breathing. Every line of her body tensed, and

he lifted his head to see her features frozen—far from the moment.

Dammit, he was an idiot times ten. He couldn't toy with her. She wasn't too young to know that what her body wanted and what her mind wanted were two separate things. And he wasn't being fair to himself either.

He released her and stumbled two steps back. Confusion warred on her features. At that moment, Lyric's despondent cry drifted from the living room.

Nola shook her head as if to regain her senses, arranged her clothing and jumped off the counter. A painful ache spread from Griffin's cock upward to clamp around his heart. Nola wasn't for him, no matter how much he wanted her to be.

"I'll see to Lyric. You can go for the day, but I want to talk to you about coming earlier," he told her.

"When should I be here tomorrow?"

His ma usually came around six-thirty, but he could push back his chores. "Seven. I'll see you at seven. And I'm sorry about what just happened. It won't happen again."

Their gazes connected for a heartbeat, but he dropped his first to stare at her little pink toes.

"See you." She moved off toward the mudroom, and Griffin issued a pent-up breath. Lyric needed him, his ma needed him. But what if he needed someone?


"What's for dinner?" Nola leaned against the counter, close to where her mother stood dicing tomatoes, onions and jalapenos.

"Spicy salsa chicken."

Nola swept her gaze over the counter at the other ingredients. Then she went to the fridge for cheese. Wordlessly, she and her mom worked to place the four cutlets in a dish then topped it with salsa and cheese.

Their silence wasn't uncomfortable, but she knew her mom was disappointed that Nola hadn't kept her job at the optometry office.

Finally, her mother spoke. "How was your day with the baby?"

Today Nola had arrived five minutes late to Griffin's, and he'd already fed and dressed Lyric. She'd looked adorable in a ruffled romper, and Griffin had combed her sparse hair into a tiny curl on top of her head.

From afar, Nola loved the idea of taking care of an infant, but when he passed the kicking bundle into her arms, worry tugged at her. In the end, Lyric had been a peach of a baby, only throwing a fit when Nola hadn't realized she needed to change a diaper until wetness seeped through onto her jeans.

And Griffin...he'd looked heartbreaking in rugged denim, boots and a flannel shirt, which he stripped off by the time he came in from his chores. Nola had drifted to the kitchen with Lyric in her arms to watch him gulp down two consecutive glasses of water.

"Want me to make you something to eat?"

He'd given her a sideways smile that jerked her off balance. "Not in our deal, is it? You take care of Lyric. I'll handle myself, thanks."

She'd nodded, fighting disappointment. After that, she'd chided herself for a solid hour. Where had the urge to care for a man come from anyway? It might be Molly's dream but hers lay with a record deal.

Nola refocused on her task and her mother. "My day went pretty well."

"No screaming baby? That's good to hear," her mother said from the depths of a cupboard, where she was bent over to drag out the blender. When they had spicy salsa chicken, they always had virgin margaritas. After spending the day reliving Griffin's lips on her nipple, Nola could use a shot of tequila in hers.

Heat sliced through her.

Molly's boot steps preceded her into the kitchen. Her sister appeared, all cowgirl smile and wide eyes, but Nola wasn't falling for the deception. Under her sister's innocent appearance was a hardcore interrogator.

She wasn't disappointed.

"How's the hunky cowboy daddy?" she drawled.

Nola leaned her elbows on the counter and propped up her chin. *Marvelously sculpted and dotted with dirt and sweat after his chores.* She'd yearned to lead him into the shower and soap him from head to toe.

"The cowboy daddy is holding it together."

Molly inched nearer, and her mother straightened. "What do you mean?" her mom asked.

"Well, he's a great dad. He had Lyric dressed and fed by the time I arrived. Then he took care of the ranch before taking his mother to a doctor's appointment. She has cancer."

Her mom's eyebrows rose. "Poor woman."

"Poor Cowboy Daddy," Molly interjected. "That's a lot of weight for a man to carry."

"For anyone to carry." Their mother adjusted Molly's romantic notions.

"No wonder he needed you," Molly said.

"Yeah, I wish I could do more. Right now Lyric takes some entertaining, but she sleeps a good portion of the day too. Griffin keeps the house tidy, so I feel as if I'm wandering around when I could be helping him."

"In the barn?" Molly waggled her brows.

Nola rolled her eyes and went to retrieve ice to feed to the blender. "I can't help but wonder what happened to the mother.

Em Petrova

I mean, what sort of woman gives up her baby?"

"Maybe it was a tragic accident and Griffin's just waiting for the right woman—" Molly stopped at their mother's pointed look.

Nola ignored her sister and shook her head. "There's a story in his past, that's for sure. And it's hard not to admire a man willing to take on the responsibility of raising a child on his own."

Both women nodded in agreement. While they mixed the margaritas they dropped the discussion. Nola and Molly set the table, and then their mother ran off to greet their daddy.

At dinner, Nola stole a peek at her father. He didn't appear angry—just a little tired.

"How was the new girl?" Nola asked around a bite of chicken laden with sour cream, salsa and cheese.

"She's catching on. And how is the nanny job?"

Nola smiled as the image of Lyric popped into her head. While Nola had fed her, Lyric's eyes seemed to grow with every suck, until they took up her entire face. "It's fine. Good pay for an easy job. The baby's a dream."

"Got you wrapped around her finger already?" Her father smiled for the first time since Nola quit, and she relaxed a little.

"Around her daddy's finger, I'd say. You should see the way he has her outfitted. The nursery looks like a bubble gum factory exploded, and the kid has a wardrobe to be envious of." Nola forked in two more mouthfuls of chicken before she realized everyone was staring at her and not eating.

"What?"

"Uh-oh," Molly said with a grin. "Sounds as if this job might be more than a means of getting to Nashville. That can mean only one thing."

Nola felt a flush creep over her throat and face. She set down her fork. "I have no idea what you're talking about."

"Did you scour the Internet for the latest in country music news today, Nola?" Molly asked.

"Well no. I didn't have time. I was working."

"Uh-huh." Molly sucked on her straw, filling her cheeks with virgin margarita.

Irritation wove through Nola. "Why can't we have alcoholic margaritas, Mom? We're all adults."

Her mother flicked her head toward the liquor cabinet. "Help yourself if it makes you feel better, but my guess is the lack of tequila isn't what has your guitar out of tune."

Molly leaned across the table. "I think it's one hot cowboy daddy."

Nola shoved away from the table, gathered her plate and dumped the contents into the trash. "I'm going to the studio to practice." Without waiting for a reply, she sailed out of the room.

As she navigated the basement stairs to her home music studio, she ground her teeth. Her family just wanted her to forget about becoming a singer and to latch onto something close to home. Simple job, married life. Children.

She wasn't ready, and she might never be. Music was in her blood. Everywhere she went people told her she should try for a music career. She wouldn't be satisfied with herself until she did.

She scooped up her guitar and sank to the edge of her chair. Her fingers worked the strings without thought, and a new tune that had been revolving in her head all afternoon started to emerge. As she toyed with the new melody, she forgot about Lyric and Griffin. By the time the words started to materialize in her mind, she was certain she walked on the right path.

*Get enough money to get to Nashville and follow my dreams.* Griffin was just a hand up to her dream. Too bad the mere thought of the rough older man made every nerve ending inside her spark.

# Chapter Five

Griffin tucked the baby monitor in his back pocket and stole out into the night. The air wrapped around him, cool and crisp. After a dirty dream of Nola bare naked and his fingers buried in her sweet pussy, he welcomed the outdoors.

Damn, that woman was trouble. Too young for him, and now that he knew she was headed to Nashville, he needed to steer clear. The last thing he and Lyric needed was to be a stop on Nola's tour.

As Griffin strode across the dew-spangled grass to the barn, his mind clicked into rancher mode. Late in the evening one of his cows had started laboring. He usually let them toil on their own for a while, checking intermittently for trouble. Now that Lyric was sleeping for her long stretch, it was the perfect time to check the cow.

The instant he stepped into the barn, he smelled trouble. Fear and pain had their own odor. And the sickness mingled with it was a dead giveaway.

He yanked the chain overhead and lit the bare bulb in the center of the barn. It cast a thin glow over the stall where the heifer was on its side, eyes rolling wildly.

"Damn." Griffin dropped to his knees in the hay and ran his hands over the cow. Her stomach rippled with the baby that was obviously trapped.

Launching back to his feet, his mind raced ahead. *Get the chain and the homemade rig used to exert pressure. Phone's in my back pocket in the event I need to call the vet.*

No, he needed to call Ma to come sit with Lyric while he

worked with the cow.

As this thought passed through his mind, his stomach clenched. His mother wasn't in any shape to make a midnight drive to Needle's Pass.

He slung the chain over his shoulder and lifted the metal rig he'd hand-crank to pull the calf. Then he fished in his pocket for his phone.

A few days ago he'd put Nola on speed-dial—in the event he needed her for an emergency, he'd told himself even as his groin ached with desire.

She answered on the fourth ring. Her throaty voice speared him with lust. Too easily he pictured her tousled hair and tank top slipping down one golden shoulder.

"Nola, it's Griffin. Can you come up?"

"I—what? Griffin?"

He smiled at the confusion in her tone. Protectiveness surged in his chest. "Yeah...Griffin. I need to pull a calf. Can you sit with Lyric?"

She made a humming noise that caused his cock to jerk. "I guess I could."

"I'll give you double pay for the extra hours. And you can sleep as long as she's sleeping."

"All right. Just give me..." She paused, and he heard items being tossed around. "Give me half an hour."

The cow's body shuddered, and Griffin stretched his lips over his teeth in his own grimace. "Thanks, Nola."

He hung up and kneeled before the cow again. He set up the rig, feeding the chain to the gear. When he cranked the handle, the chain would tighten. Now he just needed to reach inside the cow and find the calf's leg.

First he ran his hands over the calf's outline to detect the way it was laying. He'd done this often enough to know its front legs were bunched up and hindering its birth.

"Damn." He yanked off his flannel shirt and moved to the back end of the cow. "You're not gonna like me for this, but in the end, it's what you need."

The disgusting work of rooting around inside a cow's womb and searching for a foreleg took up the next few minutes. When he heard Nola's tires crunching on gravel, he swore. If he extricated himself from his project now, he might have a harder time later.

"Nola!" he called once he heard the car door close.

When she didn't respond, he called again. A moment later her footsteps sounded at the door of the barn.

"In here," he grunted as the cow's body clamped around his arm, constricting it.

"What the...?" Her boots appeared, and he squinted at her from the corner of his eye. "Yuck!"

"That's an understatement. Listen, Lyric is sleeping. The house is open. Just go on in and make yourself comfortable on the couch. There's a baby monitor in the living room already tuned to the Lyric Channel."

She smiled at that. Hell, she was still mussed from sleep, her hair loose and curling over her forehead, and her baggy sweatpants only added to her allure. "Okay, you just...do what you're doing here. I'll take care of Lyric."

He offered her a smile as he encircled the calf's leg with his fingers and tugged it downward. "Get some sleep, Nola."

She stared at where his arm disappeared into the big animal's body, disgust etched on her pretty face. "I'll try." She turned and left the barn. He listened to her crossing the lawn and the front door quietly opening and closing.

Breathing a sigh, he looked at the cow. "You and me now, babe. Let's do this thing." With a hard wrench, he guided the calf's leg forward. The cow groaned. Griffin worked for long minutes to attach the chain to the leg.

His muscles strained. From the baby monitor, he heard a snuffling noise and was instantly on high alert. He pushed away the night sounds—peep frogs and scurrying mice. Then he heard Nola's soft, soothing croon.

"Shh, baby, it's okay."

He pictured her patting Lyric's spine, calming her back to sleep. She'd probably been the one to disturb Lyric by checking on her.

Griffin smiled and secured the chain. With a grunt, he hunkered back against the side of the stall and used his flannel to wipe his hand. "We're gonna get your baby free then celebrate with a nice scoop of grain," he told the heifer.

But half an hour of cranking later, the calf was no closer to being born. Muscles burning and frustration mounting, he prodded the cow's belly, hoping to guide the baby. What he wouldn't give for a glass of sweet tea and his bed.

He fell back, out of breath from his efforts. A sweeping glance at the cow's body told him she wasn't faring well either. He worked harder. Sweat dripped into his eyes, and he blinked it away.

At that moment, Lyric's cry rang out from the monitor. He froze and shot a glance at his watch. Hell, he'd been working for two hours and it had felt like minutes. Lyric's wails echoed through the barn. A second later he heard Nola.

"What's wrong, little miss? Hungry?"

His pulse tripped at the sweet words. The baby's cries fell away as Nola obviously carried her through the house to the kitchen. A few minutes of his backbreaking attempts later, Nola's voice came through the monitor again.

She was singing.

Griffin's throat thickened. He battled the need to go to her—to put his arms around her and his child and shelter that moment. Instead he was going to have to call the vet, crop up more bills and remain in the barn until dawn seeped into the sky.

Nola's voice rose and fell in a soft ballad. He'd heard the popular song before, but her unique twist was more compelling. He placed the call to the vet and waited while Nola sang two more songs. Finally, the monitor fell silent.

Griffin swiped his damp forehead with his forearm. Telling himself over and over that Nola was too young, wasn't for him, didn't keep brand new feelings from seeping in.

Half an hour later, frustration mounted when the vet arrived and took over the battle for the calf's life.

"We'll save your cow, Turner. But we might not be so lucky with the calf," Rick said.

Griffin set his teeth together and nodded. The sun was mounting the sky. Soon he'd have to clean up and take his mother to the hospital for blood work. He'd be forced to abandon his morning routine with Lyric, and that didn't set well with him, even if Nola was doing fine.

Time ticked by, and he kept glancing at his watch.

"Got somewhere to be, Turner?" Rick asked, cranking the rig for all it was worth. The calf moved a few inches, and its foot appeared.

Griffin shook his head. "I'll see this through."

A few minutes later, the cow gave a huge push, and the calf landed in the hay, still.

"I was afraid of that," Rick said quietly.

Griffin stared at the newborn, hating that it was lost. Such a big fight to end like this.

His mother's battle might end the same. And Lyric might grow into a wild child. He may turn out to be a hopeless single parent. Might as well heap on the trouble.

"Goddammit," he grated out and got to his feet.

"I'll finish up here. You go inside. You've had a longer night than I have, Turner." Rick nodded to him.

Chest burning with anxiety, Griffin stomped out of the barn. He cleaned up with the frigid water from the outdoor spigot then went into the kitchen, where he used soap.

Around him the house was silent. Nola was feet away, sleeping on the couch, and Lyric wouldn't be up yet. Griffin stripped off his shirt and poured himself a big glass of that sweet tea he'd been craving.

After a night like this, he wished he could abuse his liver with something harder as he had in his youth, but now Lyric took care of that thought.

A shifting step made him raise his head. Nola stood there, tousled from sleep, her eyes heavy-lidded and her lips ripe.

He might not have any control over a lost calf or his mother's illness or how much Lyric disobeyed in her teen years, but dammit, he could take what he needed.

In three strides he caught Nola in his arms.

When he slanted his mouth over hers, she gave an all-over shiver. He suctioned his lips against hers, and she gulped in his scent.

This was one hell of a way to wake up. A bare-chested man in the kitchen, wearing an expression of fierce need would melt any woman, especially when she'd lain awake on his couch for hours, thinking about him.

Wanting him to do this very thing.

He took control of the kiss, swirling his tongue over hers until she grew dizzy. Her nipples puckered. When he lightly dragged his teeth over her tongue, her pussy clenched.

Swaying against him, she pressed her aching breasts to his chest. The craving for more was too strong to fight. Since that night at The Hellion, she'd only wanted to feel his rigid length gliding inside her. Now that she knew him a little better, that need was stronger.

Painfully stronger.

She looped her arms around his neck and drowned in his kisses. He rocked his erection against her lower belly—a promise to come.

Every touch, every kiss he'd given her whirled in her brain like a song—a strong man with loneliness in his eyes that vanished when he looked at her. The song could write itself, and maybe later she'd pick it out on her guitar.

Nola tangled her fingers in the longer hair on his nape. He followed her action, twisting his fist in her waves and yanking her head back. She gasped as he dropped his mouth to her throat and licked it like the most sumptuous treat.

Small squeaks emitted from her. If Molly were here she'd stand in the corner clapping with glee. Nola was female after all! *I shouldn't give in to him. I don't need a lover when I'm leaving Reedy. And he's my boss.*

Griffin raised his head and their gazes locked. In that moment, a thousand sentiments zapped between them. Her emotions somersaulted and she lost her grip on them.

"Yes," she whispered, gritty.

"Damn straight," he growled. In a fluid motion, he plucked her off her feet and spun toward the living room. The warm colors of the space blurred past her vision as she sank her teeth into his earlobe, the side of his neck.

He tugged her head and latched onto the spot above her collarbone until she felt the warmth of a bruise blossom on her skin. By the time he laid her on the sofa and stretched atop her, her panties were totally soaked.

He gripped her outer thigh and hitched her leg high around his hip. Then he angled his cock right at her pussy.

She cried out as the rock-hard length battered her through barrier of jeans and sweatpants. And she couldn't get enough of his big, bare chest. A faint spattering of hair coated his sculpted pecs. She ran her fingers through it.

"You've been tormenting me since that night in The Hellion," he said. Through her shirt he pinched her nipple.

Need clawed at her inner walls. She dug her hands into his thick, dark hair and simply felt. Nashville couldn't be farther from her right now, but she didn't care about anything but giving and taking pleasure from this man.

He peeled her T-shirt and sweats off as if he were unwrapping a prize. The look on his face made her feel more beautiful than she'd ever felt in her life. When he stared down at her in only her cotton panties and sports bra, she drank in his rugged beauty.

Hair tumbled over his blazing eyes, but he didn't bother to shake it free. She practically felt her skin tingle with excitement to feel his rough beard on her skin.

"Fuck, you're beautiful," he grated out.

She reached for him, and he brought his hot chest atop hers. The kiss of skin ignited her. He moved one big hand up her torso, dragging her sports bra up and off. He sucked in a ragged breath before burying his face in her cleavage.

Her nipples pinched hard, and she arched upward, seeking release. "Rub against me. I want to feel your skin on my breasts."

He lifted his head, a primal expression coating his features. Then very deliberately he braced himself on his arms and skimmed her tits with his chest. The warmth and sprinkle of chest hair teased her. Her eyes threatened to close with pleasure but she couldn't stop looking at Griffin.

As he slowly rubbed up and down and back and forth, their gazes remained locked. Her pussy pulsated with need.

He slipped his hand between their bodies and cupped her mound through her panties. She wished for her sexiest lace or silk underwear. Her undergarments might be plain but her first encounter with Griffin was anything but.

Slipping one thick finger inside the elastic, he studied her face. "Don't take your eyes off me. I want to watch the pleasure on your face."

She sucked in a breath as he tunneled his hand into her panties, still moving maddeningly against her breasts. Her nipples were sharp peaks dragging over his chest. When he followed the slick seam of her pussy downward, Nola stopped breathing.

Something wild sparked in his eyes, and she knew he was barely restraining himself. His cock lay against her upper thighs, a hard, enticing ridge inside his jeans. She wanted to strip him, sink over him and take her pleasure.

He stroked her closed pussy lips over and over. The action created friction against her clit, which was trapped beneath. She moved restlessly, and he flashed a grin that almost stole her heart.

"You'll get this on my terms." He pinched her pussy lips together right over her clit, applying the perfect pressure to it. More cream oozed from her folds to wet his hand. His refusal to go right for the gold heightened her awareness.

She ran her hands over his spine, reveling in the contours made by hard work. So tough yet soft. A man who could easily heft a bale of hay yet cradle his fragile infant daughter.

He squeezed Nola's nether lips around her clit again. The first sparks rolled through her system. *I'm going to come and he hasn't even really touched me.*

"Someday soon I'm going to spend all night tormenting you. But I can't wait now. I'm taking this hot pussy."

She shivered at his dark promise.

"Reach in my back pocket. Find my wallet. There's a condom." He surged upward so she could reach his ass.

Em Petrova

She felt along the hard planes of his backside and found a bulky protrusion in his pocket. She hooked her fingers around an antenna and pulled out the baby monitor.

A huff of laughter escaped him—the sexiest sound she'd ever heard. She joined him, quaking with a silent giggle as she let the monitor slip to the carpet. Then she found his wallet in the opposite pocket.

She swallowed hard under his direct gaze and plucked the foil wrapper free of the bills.

"Get my cock out and put that on me, baby. I want to feel your hands."

He leaned back on his knees just enough for her to do his bidding. She took her time, lingering over belt buckle, button and zipper. By the time she got to his boxers and reached for his throbbing shaft, she was crazy for him.

A bad-boy smirk claimed his lips. When she closed her fingers over his bare length, the smile twisted into a grimace of pleasure.

"Roll it on nice and slow. I like the build-up. The burn."

Before now she hadn't realized she did too. He shifted his weight, and she realized he was kicking off his boots. One thump then two. She stretched the condom over his straining purple head and slowly encased him in rubber.

His chest expanded around a deep breath. Was he fighting for control as much as she was? She wanted him to fill her—now.

He rolled off her and stood beside the sofa to strip off his jeans, underwear and socks. When he stood in full glory, she couldn't stand it another minute.

She climbed off the sofa and hooked her thumbs in her panties.

"No." His harsh order stopped her dead. Her heart pounded. "I'm in charge." He dropped to his knees before her and snagged the cotton of her panties in his teeth. She threw her head back as his heated breath washed over her skin.

Inch by painstaking inch he removed her last garment. Then he spread her thighs with his big hands and drove his tongue right into her soaking pussy.

She clamped off a cry and tangled her fingers in his hair. He lapped her wet folds, then burrowed deep in her channel. After a few minutes, he pulled free and glided his tongue to the top. His avoidance of her clit was driving her nuts. She rocked forward to bring him closer to it, but he circled below the hard nubbin.

He swirled his tongue all around her.

"If you don't lick my clit, I'm going to scream and wake up Lyric."

Again that huff of laughter. She caught his grin, and the knot in her belly tightened.

"I'm in charge, remember?" He slipped two fingers right into her center. No teasing this time.

Her body clenched around him, and he groaned. Pumping in and out, he stroked her pussy with his tongue—everywhere except her needy clit. She lost herself to the pressure of his fingers deep in her body and the expert way he curled them in the right spot. No fumbling, inexperienced male. He knew what he wanted and how to get it.

The orgasm rushed her out of nowhere. Electricity rocketed through her system. Her pussy squeezed hard—then contracted madly around his fingers. He added a third finger, stretching her wider, and she came apart for another long, mind-blowing minute.

Breathing heavily, she rode the waves of her aftershocks. When had she last had an orgasm that intense? Had it ever happened before?

She cupped his face. He met her gaze and very deliberately

licked her clit.

The soft, wet strum of his tongue over her aching bundle of nerves sent her soaring up the cliff of desire once more. But after a few laps of his tongue, he pulled back. He removed his fingers from her pussy and licked them clean.

She watched his tongue moving over his long digits and about came again.

"Lie down," he ordered, eyes hazy with passion.

She stretched out on the sofa, and he lowered himself right between her thighs. His muscles bulged around her. When he kissed her, she sucked in a breath. Her flavor rode on his tongue, and suddenly it was the hottest thing she'd ever known.

"Wrap your legs around me as I enter you." His voice was an untamed stallion running over her sensitive brain. He pressed his cock against her entrance.

She hooked her legs around his hips, and he entered her in one swift glide.

Again, no teasing. Just a man telling her what he wanted then taking it.

She shuddered at his invasion. His steely rod overfilled her, but damn, it felt amazing.

Griffin's eyes darkened as he moved once. Twice. "Hell, this is gonna be over too fast." A muscle ticked in the crease of his jaw.

Nola put her finger over it and surged up to kiss him. They came together in a clash of lips and bodies. He pounded her, and she bucked in return. He chased her tongue around her mouth, and she let him capture it.

Every ripple of muscle under her hands sent her flying higher. Just when she thought she couldn't feel more and survive it, he sucked her nipple.

The pressure crested, held, and she came with a wild cry.

# Chapter Six

Griffin's balls clenched tight. His cock seemed to lengthen another fraction, and he burst. Come jetted into Nola's tight sheath. He ground his teeth against a roar of bliss and clapped his hand over her mouth to keep her from making more noise.

He drove into her sweet body again and again. It had been too long since he'd lost himself so completely.

It scared the shit out of him.

He found her lips and swallowed her final coos of ecstasy. The pressure in his groin was eased, but dammit, his chest felt tighter than ever.

Sucking in a deep breath, he filled his head with her scent. *Can't happen again. She's too young. I can't risk it.*

But the thought of her never giving herself up to him again made him want to find some rope and tie her up in a neat little package to play with later.

He trailed his lips across hers, their noses brushing. Her flavors still danced in his head. A long time ago a song had materialized in his mind for Lyric's mother, but the song belonged to his child. Still, something about the tender-eyed woman beneath him made him want to belt out the ballad.

Garbled baby-talk emitted from the monitor lying on the floor and the one on the coffee table.

Nola stiffened beneath him, and he smoothed a hand down her side. Dawn had rushed into the sky during their romp on the sofa, and Lyric would be wide awake, staring at her mobile and gearing up to whine for her bottle.

Griffin planted a kiss on Nola's swollen lips. "I'll get her."

Breaking free of her body caused him more distress than he cared to admit. She looked up at him, strawberry blonde hair curling over her breasts and her cheeks reddened from the scrape of his beard.

"Damn if I don't like seeing my marks on you." Before he could say more, he scooped up his clothes and headed for his room to dress.

Stupid. So fucking good, but stupid. He disposed of the condom and cleaned up, then dressed in fresh clothes.

The phone shrilled, and he snagged it from the nightstand just as Lyric broke into loud, furious cries from the other room.

His stomach bottomed out as he saw it was his ma calling. He tucked the phone against his shoulder and answered while fumbling to close his fly. "What's up, Ma?"

"I'm not feeling too well this morning. I don't know if I can go for the blood work."

"What? No, that's not how it works. When you don't feel well, it probably means your blood counts are off and you need to have them checked. I'll be over in..." He cast a look at the alarm clock, feeling the fatigue of the last hours slam him like a Mack truck. "Thirty minutes. I've got Nola here to take care of Lyric, but I lost a calf last night and have some things to take care of in the barn."

His mother's voice was weak, and Lyric's rage drowned her words.

"Sit tight, Ma. I'll be right over, okay? I'll bring you coffee." He hung up, chest throbbing with anxiety again. Too quickly the ease he'd felt from his stolen moments with Nola vanished.

From behind, he heard her footsteps and turned. She stood in the doorway, looking disheveled and ravishing. Hell, he wanted her right now. If not for a mess in the barn, his mother needing a doctor and Lyric's hunger wails, Griffin would toss Nola into his bed and keep her there all day.

"Can you take care of Lyric?" He dug through his drawer for a pair of socks.

"That's where I'm headed."

Socks in hand, he strode to the gorgeous woman he could still taste on his lips. He branded her with a hard kiss. "Good. I'll be back in a few hours. Taking Ma to the hospital for blood work."

Nola's eyes softened. He directed an errant piece of hair behind her ear then traced her lips with the fingers he'd used inside her. Her tongue darted out, and he groaned. With supreme effort, he straightened and patted her on the bottom to propel her toward the nursery.

"I'll be back."

"I'll be wa— We'll be here." The softness in her eyes blew away like smoke, and once more he saw the drive in Nola. Maybe it was for Nashville. Unfortunately, he probably wasn't misreading her.

One thing he was sure of—the ring she'd drawn around her future didn't include him and a crying baby.

When he got to the barn, he found that Rick had cleaned up the birthing mess and given the cow fresh feed and hay. She lay on her side, resting but apparently in good health. The dead calf had been taken away.

As Griffin left the barn, his gaze snagged on a few things he needed to do. Not now. Next on the list was Ma.

Worry shifted his insides around. He needed to speak with her doctors. His ma knew her own business, but it would ease his mind. He needed order in his life—a game plan. This floating along from moment to moment made him grind his teeth.

Except with Nola. His impromptu romp with her had felt just right, in all ways. Having someone to put his arms around, to lose himself in for a few precious moments, was amazing. And now memories of her seemed to be all over his ranch.

In his truck, he saw her smooth tanned legs that night he'd driven her home from The Hellion. In his house he saw her leaning over his infant daughter. And now he wouldn't be able to enter the living room without reliving every pass of his cock through her tight walls.

His dick stirred, and he adjusted it. Nola's scent was all over him, and he longed for more.

Too bad he couldn't ignore her dreams of getting out of Reedy and pursuing a music career. Lots of young people had dreams like hers.

That was just it—she was young. He'd thrown away caution when he'd taken her body, but he didn't want to stop doing it either. He wanted her ten ways to Tuesday—from behind, riding him cowgirl style, up against the shower wall and pinned to the cool kitchen tile on a hot summer night.

But he'd only lose himself if he continued. Too easily her warm blue eyes trapped him and made his heart do little flip-flops. No, there was too much at stake. Their lovemaking couldn't be more than a one-time occurrence. They'd exorcised their demons early this morning and could both walk away from a sexual relationship.

How would she handle it? He relied on her to take care of Lyric. If she gave her resignation, he'd be screwed.

He grabbed his cell and punched a button. After two rings, his friend, Taylor, answered.

"Officer Levy."

"It's Griffin."

"I see that. As a cop, I'm pretty damn good at investigating things such as caller ID."

Griffin pushed out a laugh and relaxed a fraction. "You've been a smartass since high school, Taylor."

"Thanks. I try. What's up? You never call."

It was true that in the past four months since Lyric crash-landed in his world, Griffin hadn't gotten a free moment for beers or shootin' the shit. He could tell Taylor about his ma or the dead calf. But he found Nola's name forming on his lips.

After filling Taylor in about the situation, relief trickled through Griffin like cool water poured over his head after a day in the hot sun.

"I know this girl. Heard her sing at The Hellion. She's amazing."

"Yes," Griffin said.

"And gorgeous."

His cock throbbed. "Uh-huh."

"Pretty young thing. Tanned legs and shorty shorts."

Griffin latched onto the only word that acted as a road block. "Young."

"You like 'em young. Even as a senior in high school, you dated the freshmen."

He scuffed a hand over his face. "Damn, you're right. What's wrong with me?"

"You're a man in your prime taking an opportunity with a sweet little morsel."

"She's practically a teeny-bopper. Christ, she's so young." He groaned into the phone.

Taylor laughed. "She's not that young. Besides, you're up for the challenge, man. And she's got all the woman parts, yes?"

Griffin bit off a growl. "Fuck, yes."

"What's the problem? She's up for it, and you've been alone too long."

Leave it to Taylor to strip the situation down to basic man-talk. "Thanks for the stellar advice, as always. Come up to the ranch and help out this weekend. We'll have a beer or two."

A smile sounded in Taylor's voice. "Nothin' better than bonding over a steaming pile of manure, Turner. You got it."

Griffin ended the call and shook his head at his friend's words. Maybe he was making a big deal out of nothing when it came to Nola.

As he turned his truck down the hill leading into Reedy, his mind kicked into high gear again. Everything mounted, crushing him under the weight of responsibility and worry.

He fought for calm. The whole situation was spiraling out of control. Every cloud ran out of rain sometime, but right now, he was in the eye of the storm.

When he entered his ma's house, shock tore through him. She lay on the sofa, looking frail and ill. Her pale face was drawn.

Griffin's heart turned over. He dropped to his knees beside the sofa. "Are you all right?"

She waved a hand. Her old annoyed expression was a relief to him. "Just tired out. Help me up and we'll go let the nurses bleed me dry."

He wrapped an arm around her middle and guided her to her feet. She wobbled a little, punctuating her statement that she was tired. Every sweet memory of his ma's energy and determination to never sit idle blew away with his worst possible thoughts.

Maybe the doctors were wrong.

Could the cancer have spread?

Gut burning, he shoved away his thoughts and led his mother through the small, crowded rooms of the house. Knickknacks needed dusting and something in the kitchen smelled—dirty dishes.

He added tidying the house to his list of to-dos.

After only a few chemo treatments, his mother was a wisp of her vibrant self. He guided her into the truck and when she didn't move to buckle her seatbelt, he did it for her.

As he walked around the front of the truck, he fought a

rising panic. But by the time he got behind the wheel, he'd stomped all over it.

He was going to fight long and hard for his mother if necessary. She'd be fine. Go into remission. Live to watch Lyric crawl, walk, attend her first dance.

At the hospital, he sat with her while they drew blood. Then as they gave her a shot to boost her immune system. By the time he got her tucked into her own bed, he felt as wrung out as she looked.

When he pulled the covers over her, she placed a thin hand on his. "You're a good man."

Those tears he'd been wrangling back welled against his lashes. He smiled into her loving brown eyes. "We'll get through this. I don't like you here on your own though. Will you move into my guest room?"

Her eyelids drooped. "I'll think about it. Call me in a few hours, okay? I don't want to sleep the day away."

He almost asked why. She could spend a day resting if she damn well pleased, but that just wasn't his ma. He bent and kissed her cheek. "I will."

She snuggled under the covers, and he watched her drift off almost instantly. After he hand-washed a few dishes and ran a duster around the rooms, he cracked the blinds to let in some sunlight. Feeling better about leaving her, his mind zeroed in on Lyric—and Nola.

The drive up the steep hill to Needle's Pass had never seemed so long. His heart sped up as he set eyes on his ranch. From the outside, it appeared to be slumbering, but inside it would pulse with life.

Because his daughter was in there with a woman he could fall in love with.

He practically ran to the front door, prepared to be greeted by smiles.

Instead, all hell was breaking loose.

Nola's T-shirt clung to the perspiration under her arms as she paced the floor with the screaming baby. She'd tried everything—jiggling, singing, feeding, burping. Nothing stopped the train-whistle shrieks Lyric emitted.

Two hours into it, Nola had called her mother in tears, her hands shaking from her frazzled nerves. Her mother had calmly suggested bundling the baby. If she had colic, the tight wrap might help.

Lyric had kicked and wiggled free in seconds. Nola had wrestled the pink fuzzy blanket around her again, at which point Lyric's face turned nearly purple with rage.

Terrified, Nola had hastily unwrapped the baby and started walking again. She'd checked her diaper a dozen times. Tried to direct a nipple between the baby's lips.

She stared at the wall clock. In another hour she'd give in and call Griffin, but she didn't want to bother him while he was taking care of his mother.

And she didn't want to seem incompetent.

She did another revolution of the living room with the screeching baby on her shoulder. Every step she laid down felt weighted, and her nerves jangled like spurs on a boot-scootin' cowboy.

"Shhh, Lyric. Shhh."

The stiff baby churned her legs. Nola's hair dripped into one eye and she smelled like spit-up. Lyric's scream rose and fell beside Nola's ear, ripping at the last thread of her control. She crossed the room and picked up the phone and put it to her ear.

"Nola."

It took a heartbeat to realize Griffin's voice wasn't projecting through the receiver.

She whirled. Relief swelled in her chest, and tears sprang to her eyes.

"Oh, sweetheart."

She didn't know if he was talking to her or the baby, but she didn't care. He was here, and she could unload this screaming child.

Griffin removed Lyric from her arms and hitched her high on his shoulder. She continued to shriek, and he didn't even bat an eye. That must mean he'd dealt with this before and Nola hadn't broken the baby after all.

When he slipped an arm around Nola's waist and tugged her against his chest, she dissolved into noisy tears.

"How long has she been like this?" His soothing tone made Nola cry harder.

"Since y-you left." She dragged a disgusting breath into her nose and tried to pull herself together.

"Why didn't you call me?" His voice held no trace of judgment—only calm understanding.

"I thought I could handle it."

He gave her a little squeeze and Lyric went through a bout of hiccupping cries. He jiggled her. "Sweetheart, believe me, it takes nerves of steel to deal with Lyric's colic. You should've called."

She tipped her face up to him, and he smiled. She shoved the hair out of her eyes. "I look awful."

He shook his head. "Beautiful. In fact, your lips are like ice cream at the county fair." He swooped in and claimed them. She melted like soft serve in the summer sun.

In the past few hours she'd given herself three talking-tos about breaking things off clean with Griffin before she ended up barefoot and pregnant on his ranch. After the morning she'd spent with Lyric, the idea made her cringe more than ever. But now she took the comfort he offered—drinking in his manly scent and craving more.

He broke the kiss and gave her that crooked bad-boy smile that sent her reeling. "C'mon. I'll take care of this extremely happy baby while you shower."

"Shower?"

He grabbed her hand and led her toward his bedroom. Then with Lyric still screaming in his arms, he took the time to turn on the water and find a fluffy towel and washcloth for Nola.

She turned to him, tears still hot in her eyes. "Thank you."

"I'll lay one of my shirts on the bed for you. It will work for a few hours. Once Lyric falls asleep, I'll go out to see to the ranch then you can go on home. You've more than put in your time, but I do need you." The dark words tipped her belly.

She narrowly kept from jumping into his arms, crying baby and all. "I'll stay until you're done."

"I appreciate it." He patted her ass, lingering over the curve of her cheek. With another smile, he was out the door.

As the baby's cries drifted across the house, far from Nola, she began to calm. Steam rose around her. She stripped down and climbed under the shower spray, surrounded by the piney scents she associated with Griffin.

*Hell, I'm in trouble. Seduced by a hot shower.*

She washed away her tears, sweat and the spit-up. For long minutes she let the water course over her skin, thinking of the cowboy in the other room. A man who commanded everything he did. She still felt the evidence of his thorough command between her thighs.

She eased her fingers over her throbbing pussy. His earlier avoidance of her clit made her ache. After their wild sex, she'd been more than satisfied but now...

Was it wrong to finger herself in her boss's shower?

Why bother being prissy now? She'd already sampled the

boss himself.

She circled her hard nubbin, and electric shocks ripped through her. She leaned against the wall, parted her legs farther and stroked her pussy. Closing her eyes and inhaling Griffin's body wash boosted her fantasy.

In reality all she had to do was walk out naked and let him take control. But it wasn't fair to either of them. She'd thought this could be a fling before she left for Nashville, but now she wasn't so sure.

Besides being giving in bed, he was sweet and melted her with a single smoldering look.

Her nipples bunched as she traced a figure eight pattern over her nubbin. Juices oozed from her, and she slid one finger into her pussy—nowhere near a relief after being stretched by the man in the other room.

She rocked against her hand, letting the pressure build.

A shudder rippled down her spine. She started to breathe heavily.

The shower curtain parted, and a wall of muscle crowded her against the wall.

"Started without me, I see." His gaze burned into hers as he placed his hand over hers—and her mound. "You want me to touch you here?" He nudged her forefinger aside and pressed on her clit.

Nola's sigh rasped out. "Yes."

"Then let me." He sounded as if he'd run a marathon.

She fell against him, forehead pressed to his shoulder. When she nodded, he used two fingers to circle her straining clit. Need revved inside her—the race was on.

Who would win in this frightening game? Her body, yes. But whose heart would cross the finish line first? She'd thought she could give herself lightly, but the feeling of utter relief that he was touching her scared the fuck out of her.

With his free hand he tilted her chin and claimed her mouth. She moaned as his hot tongue lashed the inside of her mouth. He mimicked the motion of his fingers. Up and down, back and forth. Oh God, all around.

She started to peak. Her pussy pulsated.

"Not yet." He withdrew his fingers and she cried out in frustration. He huffed a laugh.

"Damn, you're so fun to tease."

She pressed her thighs together, aching for the release he'd denied her. Annoyance mingled with her want. "I was doing just fine on my own."

He arched a dark brow. Water trickled over his tanned flesh. "That so? You seemed mighty pleased when I joined you."

Yeah, she was. She met his stare and slumped against the wall, her pussy contracting. A few flicks of his finger and she'd come.

"I had no intention of getting in with you, but you looked so goddamn hot when I walked into the house a little bit ago. I couldn't quit thinking about it."

Shock staunched her need. "What?" She'd been a sniveling, disheveled mess after battling her own shortcomings with Lyric.

Griffin pinned her against the wall using his body. His hard cock jutted against her belly, tormenting her with every thick inch. He braced a hand over her head and let his lips hover above hers.

"A gorgeous woman in sweats, messy hair and looking at me with need in her eyes is the sexiest thing a man can find when he comes in the door. Now let me take care of this need."

His chest rumbled deliciously against her nipples. She wanted to beg him to ease her, make her come all over his fingers. But the words died—a ballad unsung. Instead she gripped his wrist and guided his hand to her cunt again.

"Fuck, yes," he growled, driving his tongue into her mouth

at the same time he rubbed her slick pussy.

He didn't dally around the task—finding her core and strumming it perfectly. She wrapped her fingers around his cock and rolled it through her fingers. When she dipped her fingertips low over his balls, he groaned his approval.

She lost all sense of where she ended and he began as he ran his callused fingers over her wet pussy.

He placed his mouth against her ear. "Come for me, baby. Then I'll carry you into my bedroom and worship this..." he swirled his finger over her nubbin, "...with my tongue."

His heated words sent her flying. The burning knot tightened and broke. She quivered as the most powerful orgasm she'd had yet took over. Waves of bliss slammed her.

Griffin's cock swelled in her palm, and she pumped it faster. They swayed together, kissing until she didn't know if she could stand anymore.

He slid his hand free and picked her up. The cooler air hit her skin as he burst through the shower curtain. She couldn't stop a giggle from erupting from her throat.

Angling her toward the shower again, he said, "Turn off the water, girl."

Something about the way he drawled "girl" didn't sound a bit as if he referenced their age difference. It sent streamers of warmth through her whole body.

She switched off the shower and then he swung out of the bathroom with her in his arms. He laid her still dripping on his bed and took his time staring at her.

"So damn beautiful. Ripe as a goddamn fruit for me." He eased between her legs and held them apart with his hands on her inner thighs. When he delved his tongue deep into her pussy, they shared an uncontrolled moan.

He fanned his fingers over her flesh and switched tactics, covering her clit in one intense bite. He sucked her bud, and she couldn't hold back. The sensation was too much when she was still coming down off her first high.

She came hard, bucking against his mouth and taking what she wanted. Eyes squeezed shut on the ecstasy, she didn't realize his hands were roving until he pressed his fingertip against her nether hole.

"What—? Griffin!"

"Shh, sweetheart. It's good. So good. I'll show you."

Before she could protest, he worked his finger in to the first knuckle. She squirmed, part from nervousness, part from the extreme pleasure he was forcing on her.

He planted a hand on her belly and held her down while sliding his finger in and out, opening her. He leaned forward and kissed the small patch of hair on her mound.

"Someday I'm going to take you here." To punctuate his statement, he corkscrewed his finger deeper. She cried out, her nerve endings alive in a brand new way.

"But not today," he added and slipped his finger free. Her body clenched at the loss. Her noise of despair made her flush a deep red. Griffin moved up her body and kissed her. "Don't worry. I won't make you wait too long. Now roll onto your hands and knees."

*Oh. My. God.* Still blushing furiously, she rolled onto her stomach. His footsteps moved away, and she twisted to see what he was doing. Water beaded on his shoulders and back. He opened a drawer then she heard a tearing sound.

When he turned, his big cock was fitted with a condom. The purple head was stretched. She wet her lips.

"Put that luscious ass in the air, doll."

# Chapter Seven

"What's that in your back pocket, Turner?"

Griffin turned and pierced Rick, the vet, in his gaze. He had been to the ranch so often in the last two weeks, Griffin might have to provide the man with a bedroom soon.

The calves had a virus. In two weeks, he'd lost three of them, and more were sick with the "calf scours". Everything came right back out of the poor newborns, and that meant dehydration and eventually death.

"Looks like a radio of sorts," Rick prompted.

The sleepless haze in Griffin's mind parted. Last night Taylor had finally made the trip up to Needle's Pass and the two of them had spent way too much time with a case of beer in the barn. "Oh, that's a baby monitor."

Rick fiddled with a concoction he was mixing in a big bucket. He claimed he hadn't seen a sickness this bad in a long time. The regular treatments weren't working as well as he hoped, so he'd taken to tweaking a batch of medicine. "Thought you had the little Brady girl up here as nanny."

Griffin opened his mouth to respond, but at that moment the monitor issued Nola's sweet voice. Singing again.

Rick glanced up at Griffin, a knowing smile on his face. "I see the allure of carrying the monitor."

Annoyance washed through Griffin. Yeah, he was sleeping with Nola. He was also falling for her, and that scared him almost as bad as losing all of his calves.

Using a long stick of wood, Rick stirred the mixture. "I heard Miss Brady sing once. Amazing talent. Too good for this

Podunk town." He shook his head, but Griffin felt as if the veterinarian had grabbed and shaken him.

The last thing he needed was another person telling him to stop toying with her, to let her go. His ma sometimes stayed in the guest room after chemo sessions when she was feeling too ill to stay alone. After walking in on Griffin kissing the hell out of Nola, his ma had turned and walked back to the guest room. But once alone, she'd sliced him with her tongue.

"How old is that girl?"

"Old enough to be kissing."

"You know what I mean, Griffin. You didn't learn your lesson with the last woman who was too young?"

He'd ground his teeth at the mention of Miranda. His mother rarely brought up his indiscretion or the fact he lived like a pauper so he could pay Lyric's mother off. "Nola's different, Ma."

"Is she?" She'd arched a thinning brow. "I heard tell she has dreams of going to Nashville. You gonna try to marry her before she skips town?"

"No. Just—" He fought for the words to tell her that Nola filled a hollow in his chest. Their long nights weren't only about mind-blowing sex. The time they spent talking meant more to him than anything.

In the end, his mother had simply said, "Be careful."

Nola's voice trickled into the barn. Griffin loved that she sang to his daughter. In fact, she was growing less awkward with Lyric. His daughter's diapers were only falling off about half the time now.

A grin stole involuntarily over his face.

Rick glanced up. "She sure sounds pretty."

"She does."

"I heard that because she's vying for Nashville, her daddy was pushing her to take a full-time job at his office. That's why she hightailed it outta there."

Griffin stared at Rick. Had she? Maybe he ought to spend more time in Reedy—get the gossip about the woman he couldn't keep his hands—or mind—off.

"Was this recently?" Griffin scuffed his knuckles over the hair on his jaw. Last night Nola had squealed like crazy when he ran his beard over her sensitive flesh.

Rick finished mixing and set the stick aside. "Few weeks ago, I'd say."

Griffin's stomach knotted. That crazy feeling that the world was tilting plagued him again. "You gonna be all right for a few minutes?"

"Sure."

Without another word Griffin strode from the barn. The sun peeked over the roof of the house. From the monitor in his back pocket a wail sounded, and he pushed himself faster.

He entered the house quietly, aware his ma was still asleep at this early hour. He didn't bother to toe off his boots but headed straight for the nursery.

The cries increased, and a splashing sound accompanied the noise. He veered toward the bathroom instead. Nola had the baby in the mesh infant seat in the tub, but she leaned back on her ankles, staring at Lyric with horror on her face. Lyric churned her arms and legs, face pink with a yell.

"She's not a mermaid," Griffin drawled from the doorway.

Nola jerked, and her face scorched. She picked up the washcloth and swirled it in the shallow water.

"Lyric giving you trouble?"

"Well, it's just that...she started to roll."

Griffin's chest burned with a laugh. Biting his lower lip to keep from making Nola feel bad, he drifted forward. "Yeah, she's been doing that. She can roll to her belly but still hasn't figured out how to get onto her back again. Just wash her up quick and she'll be too annoyed to roll. She hates her bath."

Something like relief moved in Nola's eyes. "She cries for you a lot?"

"Well, she lets me know when she disapproves. I just quiet her with a song."

Nola froze. "A song?"

"Yeah." He kneeled beside Nola at the edge of the tub and stared down at Lyric. She flapped her arms at his presence. He stared into his daughter's eyes and crooned the first verse to her song. As he noticed how still Nola had grown, awareness seeped into him. His voice was nowhere near as refined as hers. But he sang from the heart, and he figured that was just as good.

Nola's shoulder brushed his, and a shiver ran through her into him. He stopped singing and directed his gaze at her.

Her lips were parted, her eyes stormy with an emotion he couldn't name. "Who wrote that song?"

He dipped his head. "I did." Reaching into the tub, he caught Lyric's hand. She folded her fingers tightly around his thumb.

Nola's voice was breathy. "I didn't know you were a songwriter."

"Nah, I'm a rancher."

"But the melody—the lyrics. They blend perfectly."

He blushed. To cover the moment he removed the washcloth from Nola's hand, added soap and wiped Lyric down. She cooed when he washed her hair, and Nola giggled.

Griffin's throat constricted. Being with her in this way felt deceptively like a family. But Rick's words—and his ma's too— whirled in his brain like a dust storm.

"You worked with your father before you came here."

She pivoted her head to look at him. Their lips were inches apart. If he closed the gap, he could forget about anything but

96

her sweet taste. But dammit, he couldn't continue to fool himself.

She wasn't his.

She wasn't Lyric's.

"I did," she said.

He grabbed the towel off the corner of the sink and unfolded it. Then he lifted Lyric out of the tub and wrapped her in the terrycloth. The baby giggled as he rubbed her dry. Without waiting for more from Nola, he launched to his feet and carried Lyric into the nursery.

Nola drifted in. "You never asked where I worked. Is it a problem?"

"Nope." He placed Lyric on the changing table and grabbed one of the fresh outfits he kept there. Then he hooked her little ankles in one of his hands and lifted her bottom to diaper her.

Nola came to stand at his side. "You're good at that."

He looked up at her begrudging tone. "I'm good at a lot of things, but with you I'm floundering, Nola."

She blinked. "What?"

"You're going to Nashville. Why let me keep seducing you before you go?"

She took a hasty step away, shoulders suddenly tense. "I don't think I'm the only one at fault."

"You could have said no. But you let me—" He almost blurted "fall" and bit it off before he embarrassed himself. Lyric started to roll, and he pinned her with a hand on her belly. She giggled.

"You knew I plan to leave Reedy. I thought you just wanted a romp before I go."

He shot her a glare. "Woman, I don't call what we're doing a romp."

She backed up another step. "What is it?"

He opened his mouth to speak, but her expression said she

didn't want to know. And hell if he thought it was a good idea to tell her that she felt as if she'd always been in his life, that he wanted to share Sunday picnics with her, wanted to see her clothes in his goddamn closet.

Where a younger man might take years to come to this decision, Griffin took weeks.

He turned back to Lyric and stuffed her into a pink smock and soft cotton jeans.

"Griffin, I have two hundred fifty CDs out with agents and music professionals all over Nashville. When I answered your ad, I had twenty bucks in my pocket, but I didn't want to earn money for my trip from my father. He was getting attached to me in his office. I had to leave."

*What if I'm attached to you in my house, my nursery, my goddamn bed?*

He made a quiet noise in his chest and placed Lyric on his shoulder. Looking right into Nola's eyes, he said, "This thing we have—it's not ending."

She eased back another step. He followed her until she was pressed against the Tickle Me Pink wall. She twisted her hands. Then as if giving in, she placed her palms against his chest. Lyric kicked at her fingers, but Nola didn't budge.

Determination spread through him. He could back off and endure his bleak existence as a single dad and his mother's caretaker. But Nola made him feel like a man, and he wasn't going to throw that away.

"I can't give up my dreams—" she started.

He swooped in and claimed her lips. She opened to him, and he snaked his tongue into her hot depths. Groaning, he pulled her against him. Lyric wiggled, but he ignored her for the moment and lost himself in Nola's delicious response.

Damn, she was honey fresh from the comb. Her youth had never seemed so apparent, but he was going to hogtie the problem. She could go to Nashville as long as she came back to him.

Nola made a humming noise that instantly aroused him. Lyric flailed until she gained a handful of his longer hair, and he withdrew from the kiss.

Nola stared at him, eyes hazy.

"Come to me when Lyric falls asleep," he said.

She let her hands drop from his chest. "I have to go home tonight. I can't stay again."

He pinched a tendril of her strawberry-blonde hair and rolled the silk between his callused fingers. "You say that until I slide my fingers under this tiny denim skirt you torment me with and find your pussy waiting for me."

She drew a hitching breath.

He released her hair and squeezed her hip. "I bet you're not wearing panties in hopes I found your surprise."

A pink flush climbed her throat and cheeks. "I'll come to you when Lyric falls asleep."

"That's my girl," he whispered, handing over the baby. As he left the house, triumph made his heart pound.


Nola tiptoed into the nursery to check on Lyric one more time. After putting her down for her afternoon nap, she'd rinsed out bottles and hand-washed a few dishes, all the time throwing looks out the small kitchen window.

Griffin was out there waiting for her.

The baby slept in her crib, surrounded by pink checkered and polka-dotted bedding. Her dark hair curled on the back of her head, tiny whorls that might mimic Griffin's if his hair were cropped short.

Lyric gave a sigh, and Nola's heart expanded. Griffin did the same thing in his sleep.

God, she was in trouble. The man was firmly yanking her into his world. Leaving would be a wrench, but she couldn't think about that now. Not when Lyric was asleep and his words barreled through her head. *Come to me when Lyric falls asleep.*

The infant's sleep schedule was changing since Nola had started caring for her. She wasn't taking a long afternoon nap and instead falling asleep earlier in the evening.

*That means Griffin and I can watch the sun set.*

The romantic notion and the weight it carried wasn't lost on her. Hell, in some ways they were already like an old married couple, buttoning up the house together at night before falling into his big, plush bed. Sleeping wrapped in each other's arms after she'd told her parents she was sleeping on the couch.

While these thoughts scared the shit out of her, it didn't stop her from wanting him. She left the nursery and stole through the house.

The cool evening air felt good. Nola filled her lungs to bursting with the fresh country smells. Wildflowers and newly mown hay. The ranch was picturesque before her, and she let her gaze flit from barn to animals to fence to outbuilding. Each one kept up by Griffin's own hand.

How, she had no idea. He worked alone, cared for Lyric and his ma. He even cooked.

Maybe Nola could take that chore over for him. When he came into the house after a back-breaking day of work, he deserved a hot meal awaiting him.

She lengthened her strides and crossed the turf between house and barn. Griffin had spent countless hours out there recently. The calves were sick, dying, and concern etched itself all over his handsome features.

When she stepped into the barn, her heart lurched at the sight of him leaning heavily on a stall door, head in his hands.

"Griffin." Her voice sounded rough with emotion.

He scrubbed his hands over his face—to erase his emotion? Slowly he turned and gave her a smile. The way he raked his gaze over her, starting at her ponytail and moving over tank top, denim skirt, her tanned legs and ending at her pink toenails, made her feel more feminine than she ever had before. Desired. That was the word.

Without thought, she rushed toward him. He caught her, whirled and slammed her against the nearest barn wall. The prickly wood through her thin tank top inflamed her.

"Goddamn, you're a beautiful woman," he growled a split second before crushing his mouth over hers. Tall, dark and handsome mingled with mint, musk and passion. He thrust his tongue between her lips and stole her control.

She rubbed against him wantonly. Her nipples were sharp peaks, aching for his pinch. He wrapped her ponytail around his fist and yanked her head back. The delicious strain of her hair on her scalp made her pant.

Griffin lowered his mouth to her chin, nipping the underneath before tracing a line with his tongue to her collarbones. She gripped his head and guided him, gasping as he raised gooseflesh with his kisses.

"Your throat needs more kisses." He bit into the side of her neck. Fuck, she was going to have a hickey and be forced to wear a turtleneck in the middle of the Wyoming heat wave, but she didn't care.

Her pussy flooded. He was right earlier—she wasn't wearing panties. She'd had visions of bending over in front of him so he could get a good view of her bare cheeks and her slash of wetness between her legs.

"And your tits." He cradled each, fanning his thumbs back and forth with maddening slowness. She squeezed her eyes shut on the sensation.

When he pinched each tight bud hard, she cried out.

"Go ahead and scream out here, baby doll. No one is going to hear you."

He always kept a baby monitor with him while outside the house, and it hummed pleasantly from his back pocket. He rolled her nipples between his strong fingers until her legs shook. Juices oozed down her inner thighs.

He lifted his head, and she opened her eyes. His wide, full mouth was twisted. He thoroughly enjoyed seeing her undone, and that only made her feel more beautiful.

Reaching into her neckline and plunging his fingers right into her bra cup, he flashed that grin that made her heart race. "Scream my name."

With that, he dipped his head and sucked her nipple into his flaming-hot mouth. She squealed as he drew on her needy bud while swirling it with his tongue. She dug her fingers into his hair and tugged him down harder on her.

His growl of appreciation sparked her need. The knot in her belly tightened painfully, and she clamped her legs together to hold the sweet ache in place. Never wanting it to end.

He popped her other breast free and switched his tormenting kiss to it. The dark pull was doing things to her insides, unraveling her in ways she didn't know possible. "Griffin," she whispered, too raggedly.

He snaked his tongue around her pink bud. The faint touch tormented her. He scraped his teeth over her hard nipple, and she convulsed in his arms. "Who do you want to touch you?"

She threw her head back and cried it to the rafters. "Griffin!"

"God, you can't begin to know the things you do to me." He opened his mouth over her nipple and drew her down in a haze of sexual pleasure. Her inner walls were starting to clench and release. She moved restlessly.

Still licking, lapping and sucking her nipples in turn, he

stroked a rough hand up her outer thigh. He burrowed right under her skirt. When he found only skin where cotton should be, he increased his tongue action on her straining bud.

Nola slipped her hands over his shoulders. She reached between his shoulder blades and bunched the damp cloth of his T-shirt. He released her breast long enough for her to yank his shirt off. Before she could lose herself in the rugged beauty of his chest and powerful shoulders, he pressed his steely heat to her bared breasts.

"I want you naked, but not against this hard wall." Reaching around her hips, he claimed her mouth again as he lifted her. She closed her eyes and let him put her where he wanted.

He could do anything he wanted. Even take her in the ass today. Since the moment he'd probed her sensitive nether hole with a finger, she couldn't stop craving more fullness there.

When he laid her on something soft, she opened her eyes. Above, a watery light filtered in through a vent. The scents of animal and clean hay reached her. But the musk of the man grinding his thick erection into her thigh was everything.

"I was right—no panties. Jeezus, baby." He nudged her wet folds with two fingers. His pupils dilated as he screwed them into her soaking channel.

Nola parted her thighs farther and rocked her hips against his assault.

"You're so fucking wet for me. How long have you been thinking about this?" He added a third finger and strummed her swollen clit with his thumb. The first contractions raced through her cunt, and cream soaked him.

"All day. You made me wait so long." Her words sounded like a pouting child, but he only curled his fingers to find her G-spot.

Tendrils of heat wove through her body and created a tighter knot. God, the fullness of his fingers stretching her, the

103

pressure of his fingertips drove her wild.

She bucked upward, seeking more. Suddenly he pulled free of her body. She followed him and mewled with discontent.

His huff of laughter was a rich cloak surrounding her. Her heart pattered as he hovered near. His dark hair obscured one eye, but primal want burned from the other chocolate brown eye.

"I want you to wrap your pretty little lips around my cock, baby doll. I want to feel the head of my erection against the back of your throat. Think you can take me?"

"Y-yes."

She'd never given him oral. In fact, she had little experience. Her fumbling efforts in the backseat of a sedan after prom didn't teach her anything about how to pleasure a man.

She touched a white hair weaving through the dark growth on his jaw. He'd probably had countless women suck him off, but she wanted him to remember her.

When she spoke, her voice was hoarse. "Where do you want me?"

Satisfaction flashed in his eyes. His lips twisted into more of a bad-boy smile. "Right there, lying down and spread out, your perky tits out and ready for my hands. And I'm going to drive my fingers into this wet pussy while you take my cock between those pretty lips."

His gritty language made her want to sin day and night. He stood at her head and ran a hand down her belly to her pussy. She reached for him. He let her unbutton his worn Wranglers and reach into his boxer briefs. As she pulled his shaft free, a shudder rolled through him. She watched the carved muscles of his abs flex, and power filtered into her.

With sure strokes up and down his arousal, she stared up at him. He held her gaze. When she reached a certain spot on the underside of his cock, his eyes would flutter until they almost closed.

"Guide it to those sweet lips, gorgeous girl. Let me feel how hot and wet your mouth is."

"Mmm." She eased him toward her lips, and he positioned his body close, leaning over her to get the right angle. She didn't want to think about him ever doing this with another woman. Right now she wanted to be the only thing in his mind.

Holding his gaze, she opened her lips. He eased his thick shaft in. He was bigger than she'd thought. The head was fat and red with pent-up lust. She clamped her lips over it and held onto him.

He growled in response and his hips churned. He slipped his cock deeper into her mouth. She reveled in the salty flavor of the man and moved her tongue over his flesh to get more.

"Jeezus hell fucking shit." He gripped the side of her face, trapping her hair under his hand, and pushed deeper. She continued to look up at him, unable to glance away from the acute pleasure on his face.

She relaxed her mouth to take every velvety inch of him. The way he stretched her jaw felt good, and she hummed her pleasure.

"Goddamn motherfuck."

The harsh curses and the look on his face spurred her on. She moaned around him. With a hard thrust, he brought his cock deep into her mouth at the same moment he reached down her body and found her soaking wet pussy.

She cried out around his girth as he burrowed his fingers into her. Tipping her hips, she urged him toward that spot he knew so very well.

He eased his cock out and thrust back home. A salty drop of come hit her tongue, and she sucked. Wanting to drain him. To see those little creases of worry around his eyes dissipate even for a few minutes.

Em Petrova

He circled her G-spot, and she flooded with fresh arousal. They shared a groan, and he did it again. And again. She grasped his ass and drew him forward, wanting to take him as deeply as possible.

"Gorgeous girl. Hair mixing with the hay, your eyes wide for me, this pussy hot for me." He sank between her lips and plunged his fingers into her sheath five times...six. Her inner thigh muscles started to quiver, and her pussy clenched.

"Fuck yeah. My cock disappearing between your sweet lips and my fingers into your other lips... I can't hold off much longer. Give me your orgasm. Now." He pressed hard against her inner wall, and her whole body spasmed.

"Now. Now. Now." Every naughty grunt he issued was music to her heart. Her pussy heated, then she tipped over the edge. With a cry around his fat cock, she came. He stiffened, and his mouth contorted to an O of bliss. His cock sank a millimeter deeper into her throat, and hot jets of come filled her.

She swallowed reflexively. He pistoned his hips, finger-fucked her and gave her more satisfaction than she would have imagined. Giving back to him in this way felt right.

Breathing heavily, he kept his fingers buried in her core but pulled his cock from her mouth. She ran her tongue around her lips to capture the last of his essence.

"Holy hell, baby doll." He dropped his head to her shoulder and drew gulping breaths. She rubbed his nape, realizing just how vulnerable he was for all his masculinity and determination.

His mouth was near her ear, and his breathing started to slow. A snippet of a melody soughed softly from him, and her heart jerked. Fear raced off through the fields of her soul as she realized the hummed tune was a bar from the song he'd sung for Lyric.

*Only one lyric important enough to sing to you.*

Fuck. She had to get to Nashville before it was too late.

106

# Chapter Eight

Crumbles of earth clung to the backs of Griffin's hands as he finished burying the calf. He locked his jaw against a roar. He only had one calf left. The illness had wiped them out. That meant no new cows to auction at the end of the summer. No money coming in.

He had a big installment due for Miranda's schooling. In another year, she'd be finished, but for now, he was stretched to the max. Add vet bills and extra gas money it took to drive into Reedy almost daily with his ma, and he was about to buckle under the financial weight.

And Nola…it almost felt wrong to pay her. He was so entrenched in their relationship, and she was so much more than Lyric's caretaker to him.

He rocked back on his heels and stared at the grave. Two more cows were ready to drop calves, but dread filled him at the thought. As soon as the newborns burst into the world, the fight would be on.

With a sigh, he gained his feet and grabbed the shovel. Heading for the outbuilding, he scoured the grounds for a glimpse of Nola. Sometimes she'd come outside with a thermos of scalding coffee for him, but not today.

No, after their shared release in the hay, she'd withdrawn. Silently she'd returned to the house, and his chest had tightened further with fear.

He put away the shovel and washed up in the outdoor sink. He needed to shower before taking Ma into the hospital, but the position of the sun told him he was already running late.

When he entered the house, he found his ma sitting at the kitchen table, dressed to go.

"How did you get here?"

"Martha Gallagher was driving up to visit a friend and I hitched a ride with her."

"When?"

"An hour or so ago."

"Am I running that far behind?" he asked.

"A lot behind, son. We missed my appointment."

"What?" He shot a look at the wall clock and found it an hour later than he'd guessed. "Fuck, I'm sorry. Someone should have hollered for me. Can we reschedule?"

"I'm not sure. I don't want to go anyway. Let's forget about it for today—"

He stomped across the room to the phone. "Like hell." Neither of them was giving up that fight. He punched a few buttons on the phone. Just as it started to ring, Nola entered with Lyric.

She avoided his gaze, and he pressed his lips into a tight line to keep from barking at her. Someone answered the phone in the chemo center, and he opened his mouth to speak at the same time Lyric gave a peal of rage.

He whirled on Nola. She was cradling the baby instead of hoisting the infant over her shoulder so Lyric could look around. Of course Lyric was upset.

He covered the phone with his hand. "Dammit, Nola, she hates being held that way."

Shock passed over her face, and he could feel his ma's sharp glare. He spun away from all three difficult females and spoke to the woman on the phone about a new time for his mother to come in.

When he had a new time in his head, he turned back. Nola had Lyric on her shoulder, and the baby's bright eyes blinked at him over her stiff shoulder. Annoyance mounted in his chest.

He glanced at his mother, who gave him a withering look of disapproval. He almost felt his balls draw up into those of an eight-year-old boy's. He started to speak, then caught sight of an envelope lying on the kitchen table—the university logo apparent.

The goddamn bill came early.

"Nola, get the bottles made for the day, and make sure I have enough diapers to get me through tonight. I think we're running low."

Out of the corner of her eye, she glared at him. "I'll do that," she said coolly.

"Griffin, you're being an ass this morning." His ma's observation was a twig snapped in his chest. Lyric squealed again, and while he knew she just wanted him, he stormed across the kitchen and snapped her out of Nola's arms.

The woman tilted her chin up at him, anger coating her delicate features. She set her fists on the narrow spot above her hips. Sparks of anger shot between them, then she grunted and whirled away.

"Griffin—"

He ignored his mother and chased Nola, Lyric flapping happily in his arm. That his daughter smelled faintly of Nola wasn't lost on him.

In the living room he snagged Nola's shoulder and spun her to face him. Something in her eyes shifted.

Hurt.

Guilt swelled in his chest.

"If I'm not doing a good job, then let me go. I have places to be anyhow." The hard glitter in her eyes told him exactly what she was talking about.

"You want Nashville, then do it. Why wait around? I'm sure I've paid you enough money by now to get a flight and a hotel for a while."

She issued a disgusted noise and continued through the living room to the duffle bag she'd been keeping there. Her personal items warmed him every time he spotted them.

With jerky movements she zipped the bag and hefted the long strap over her shoulder. "Fine. I'll go home and make arrangements now."

Every cell in his body screamed for him to stop being an asshole, get a grip and tell her to stay. He couldn't do this without her, but his need for an employee had morphed into his need for a soul mate. If it was going to end, this was the best time—before he went out and added to his debt by buying a goddamn ring.

"I'll go into town and get you the money I owe for this week if you want to stop by tomorrow for it."

"Yeah." Her words were flat, her eyes dead. "I'll do that."

She strode back to the kitchen. He drifted to the doorway in time to see her wrap an arm around his ma's frail shoulders. "Take care, Alice."

Without a backward glance, Nola walked out of his kitchen. Out of his house. Out of his life.

His throat constricted, and he buried his nose against Lyric's throat, battling his own stubborn anger.

When the crunch of her car tires could be heard no longer, his mother finally spoke. "Ever hear that saying about it not being important how you weather the storm but how you dance in the rain, son?"

He could barely force a response past the knot in his throat. "No."

"Well, you aren't dancin'." She got up and walked away too, leaving him alone with his daughter, who promptly pooped her pants.

Nola's country music ringtone blared through her bedroom. She flailed an arm out of her covers and batted at the cell phone on the nightstand. It stopped ringing.

Thank God. She dropped her head back to the pillow just as it started blaring again.

Molly's fist vibrated the wall between their rooms. On the opposite side of the room, a resounding bang that could only be her father's fist sounded, followed by her mother's, "Nola!"

She grabbed for the phone before her family had to hide her body. "It's three o'clock in the morning. What the hell can be so important?" she answered the phone without glancing at the caller ID.

"Nola."

Her heart spasmed at Griffin's voice. Everything came back to her—his ugly behavior the previous morning, how he'd snapped at her and made her feel as if she was incompetent with Lyric. As if she didn't feel incompetent enough.

"I need you. It's Lyric. She rolled off my bed, and I—I'm freaking out."

"I can hear that. Did you pick her up?" Now she was giving him advice on parenting? What a fucked-up change of pace.

"Of course I picked her up! And she quit crying already, but I'm afraid she has a head injury or something."

Fear tingled in Nola's fingertips. "Why did you have her in your bed?"

"I just wanted to feel her close to me," he said. But Nola heard: *I missed you.*

"I'll be right there. If she starts acting strange, call 911. Did you call your mother?"

"No, she's still in the hospital. She passed out during her chemo session."

"Hell. Griffin, I'll be there in twenty minutes."

"Thought it takes you half an hour to get to Needle's Pass."

She glanced down at her nightshirt. She could throw on some jeans and flip-flops and not bother tidying her hair. "Give me twenty minutes, but don't expect my teeth to be brushed."

She heard gratitude and a hint of a smile in his voice. "Thank you, baby doll."

She didn't respond but ended the call. Then she put on those jeans and flip-flops, too aware of how many hours it had been since he called her baby doll.

Navigating the twisty road to Needle's Pass was harrowing enough in the daylight. At night, with animals bounding across the road in front of her and a nice haze of fog at the top of the mountain, Nola's grip on the steering wheel left her knuckles white.

While she drove she ran through what she knew about head injuries, which was just about as much as she knew about infants. Still, the thought of Lyric being hurt made Nola's stomach flutter.

And Lyric's poor cowboy daddy, up there alone, worried for his mother and frightened by his daughter's fall...

Nola navigated the car up the long gravel drive. By the time she reached the house, her knees were shaking. She could open that door and find anything. She wasn't prepared for this sort of responsibility.

*I'm only a friend.*

She steeled her nerves and went inside. "Griffin!"

He came out in only his boxers, hair mussed, eyes frantic.

Nola's stomach plummeted to her manicured toes. She rushed forward. "What is it?"

He grabbed her forearm and hauled her through the house to his bedroom. The bed was piled with pillows, but on closer inspection she realized Lyric was in the center of a pillow fort.

Nola hurried forward and climbed onto the bed. Lyric was fast asleep, her face just a little pink from crying. Nola watched her chest rise and fall rhythmically for a long minute. "She looks okay."

"I...I think she is." He sounded so unsure, so unlike himself that Nola caught his hand and pulled him onto the bed with her. He searched her eyes. Then with a gruff noise, he dropped his head to her shoulder and buried his nose against her neck. He brought his arms around her in a crushing grip.

Her heart leaped.

"God, Nola. Doing this all on my own sucks. She's not a calf. I don't know if she's broken or well, if she'll need birth control at sixteen or I should pull out the shotgun to greet her first boyfriend."

Nola's belly moved with her quiet laugh. She ran her hands over his nape and shoulders. "You don't need to worry about that yet."

His lips glided over her throat, inflaming her instantly. Her fingers twitched in his hair. "Everyone says it'll go fast. What about bike wrecks and broken bones? What about puberty? I don't know anything about periods and bras."

Nola's smile stretched. The worries sounded odd coming from the big strong cowboy. She started to say, "I'll tell her about periods and bras." But clamped her lips shut.

Then she considered reassuring him that Lyric's grandmother would tell her. But Alice might not be around for it.

"It's going to be okay," she said instead.

He suddenly grasped her and tilted her into the mattress, outside of the pillows that surrounded Lyric. Griffin held Nola like a drowning man. Her heart panged.

"I'm so damn sorry for yesterday, baby doll. I'm no good alone. I'm no good at long nights."

"Is that why you brought Lyric in?"

"Sort of. She's all I really have when it comes down to it.

Ma's so sick. The doctors don't know if they can get her to a good place for the surgery. Then we still have a long road of more chemo ahead. And you're off to Nashville."

Her eyes burned, but she fought the stinging drops there. "Griffin..." she stroked his rough jaw, "...what happened to Lyric's mother?"

He released her and rolled away as if he couldn't think about someone else and hold her. Tension flowed through Nola's veins.

Griffin slung an arm over his eyes and released a short sigh. "She's out of the picture."

"Meaning...?"

"I thought she and I had a good thing. But then she got pregnant. I asked her to marry me."

Nola's heart constricted. "Then what happened?"

"She said no and scheduled an abortion."

Her eyes flared open. "What?" She shot a look at the sleeping baby, imagining a world without a girl named Lyric. She shook her head in shock.

Griffin removed his arm and looked at Nola. "It's true."

"What did you do?"

A muscle in the corner of his jaw jumped. "I stormed into the abortion clinic and did the only thing I knew to do."

Her mind raced over the vision of him stomping past nurses and intimidating doctors. "How did you stop her, Griffin?"

He heaved another sigh. "I blackmailed her. Promised to pay her way through college if she had the baby. She signed off Lyric and I took over from the day she could leave the hospital."

Nola stared at him in awe. He had major guts to take on the responsibility of being a single dad. Sleepless nights, bouts of colic, making bottles and cleaning diaper blow-outs. He was just...wow.

114

"So you're paying for Lyric's mom's schooling."

"Yes. And housing. It's worth it but—" He scrubbed a rough hand over his face. "It's draining my checkbook."

"And now your calves are sick."

"Dying. All gone. I have those two cows about to calve soon but they'll probably die too. I usually keep a few to add to the herd and sell the rest."

She folded her lips together. The fact she was draining him financially too wasn't lost on her. Her expression must have broadcasted this because he rolled toward her and gathered her in his arms.

"Don't think it for a moment. The money I pay you for taking care of my daughter is well-spent. Besides, I can't wear a front-pack baby carrier while shoveling manure. I need you here, baby doll." His gaze bore into hers. "You do a great job with her, even if I was an ass yesterday about it. She loves you."

They both looked at the baby. She'd kicked free of the light blanket and her pink toes peeked out. Something in Nola's heart shuddered—she longed to stroke those soft toes.

Griffin needed her. With no caretaker, he'd be in a heap of trouble. Nola would still go to Nashville. Just not yet.

But she had to distance herself a bit from the family. She was steadily falling into their clutches. She'd also been neglecting her music. Her guitar hadn't been strummed for days, and lately the only time she'd loosed her voice was to sing to Lyric.

Secretly she knew Griffin could hear her over the baby monitor. Deep down she wanted to show off, but she restrained herself. It wasn't a radio broadcast. But she missed singing to an audience.

The following night was karaoke at The Hellion, and she'd be there. Maybe she'd stop at home and grab her guitar so she could keep it here, play while Lyric was asleep. At least she wouldn't get rusty.

"Don't leave, Nola." Griffin's voice was gritty. His soft, dark eyes seduced more than the man's full lips and scent.

"I'll stay and help out," she said. *For now* reverberated between them, unsaid.

He leaned in and gently brushed his lips over hers, slowly burning her deliciously with his beard. When he pressed his tongue into her mouth, she gasped and opened to him fully.

He slanted his mouth over hers, drinking deeply but infusing her with more emotion than she'd ever felt. It scared the fuck out of her, but she couldn't fight it. Not right now, when he'd just opened up to her. That glimpse into his brain only endeared him more to her.

As he pulled away and tucked her tight against his muscled form, she grew weighted with fatigue. In a few hours Lyric would be up and raring to go. And if Nola was going to keep her eyelids open long enough to belt out a song or two to the rowdy crowd at The Hellion, she'd better get some rest.

Griffin's warm breath washed over her temple, lulling her. Being with him was like sliding into a heated bath after a long, hard day.

# Chapter Nine

Griffin's morning glory throbbed against Nola's rounded backside. Her hair fell forwarded, affording him access to the tasty side of her throat. He stared at the spot he loved to lick for a long minute, deciding whether it was a good idea to wake her.

Dawn was already lightening the sky. Before long Lyric would be up, and the cows would need tending. He had a small window of time to take what he wanted.

And he wanted her, goddammit.

He opened his mouth over her golden throat, probing the soft depression behind her ear with his tongue.

She squirmed against him and sighed. He continued his ministrations, grasping her hip lightly to pull her ass into his erection. When she awakened he felt each inch of skin come alive. She rocked against his cock, and he bit off a growl.

Behind them, Lyric slept away in the center of his bed. Sleeping better there than she ever did in her crib. But he wasn't about to start bad habits. He wanted Nola in his bed more.

He captured Nola's earlobe in his teeth and wiggled it back and forth. Her breathing hitched. "Let's roll onto the floor," he whispered.

She gave a nod, her soft hair tickling his nose. Then together they eased themselves to the thick carpet. She tried to twist into his arms, but he held her back to his front, unwilling to give up her ass just yet.

In the back of his head, a craving had begun the other day when she'd let him finger her there. He wanted to know every

Em Petrova

inch of her body, to taste it, and that including licking a spot she might not agree to.

He cupped her ass cheek and squeezed. She stifled a groan. He swirled the letter N over her skin, caressing her ass lower and lower until he breached the crease between thigh and pussy.

She stopped breathing. He ran a finger along the seam of her pussy, annoyed by the amount of clothes between them. He wore only boxers but she had slept in a nightshirt and jeans.

Griffin reached around her front and tugged up her shirt. She moved where she needed him, giving access to her button and zipper. He bared her lower belly to his palm and sucked on her throat.

She bore his mark from the evening in the barn. Seeing that small red spot on her tender flesh spurred a primal need for more. Hell, he wanted to nip, bite and rub his jaw all over her until no one would look at her and not know she belonged to him.

He wiggled her jeans down her hips, dragging her panties with them. She kicked her feet free with a whisper of fabric. As he eased her nightshirt up and over her bare ass, she sucked in a harsh breath.

His cock stretched another fraction to an impossible length. He could smell her arousal—that dark, musk of feminine need. His mouth watered for her.

Slipping his fingers over her ass to her secret heat between her thighs, he drowned in images of doing this every day for the rest of his life. Of having her every possible way, bending her to his desires and teaching her how much she needed it too.

She cooed when he found her soaking center. He probed her entrance with one finger. He circled it then ran the tip right up to her straining button. He tapped it, and she bucked.

"Don't make a sound," he breathed against her ear. Then before she could understand his plan, he slid down her body

118

until her ass was right against his face. He kissed the golden cheek. God, she smelled like vanilla body wash. Felt incredible.

And he was going to damn well taste her. Now.

With his finger still on her throbbing clit, he used his other hand to part her ass cheeks. She didn't protest. The little puckered nether hole beckoned to him. He didn't hesitate—just snaked out his tongue and licked it.

She thrashed, trying to turn, to make him stop, but he held her fast by pressing the hood over her clit back and finding her needy center.

She fell still, and he took immediate advantage by plunging his tongue into her ass. Her personal flavors coated his tongue, and he rumbled his joy. He stretched her with his tongue, pressing deeper and deeper while fingering her pussy. After a few minutes she started to move against him, rising and falling under his tongue.

He sent a finger into her tight pussy and kept his middle finger on her button.

"Griffin," she panted.

He reluctantly lifted his head. "Don't fight me. I'm going to do this again and again, but next time we'll be outside. I swear I won't stop until the people in Cheyenne know my name." Then he dove back in.

She tipped forward and pushed slightly onto her knees. He ran his tongue over each ridge of her rosette until her legs quivered and juices dripped over his hand. He lapped at her another ball-clenching second before inserting one of his fingers into her hot body.

The first pulsations around his hands crazed him with lust. Her pussy walls gripped him, and her ass hugged him perfectly. He pumped his fingers deep, deeper. Then he curled his finger in her pussy and replaced his finger in her ass with his tongue.

She burst with a muffled cry. Her body jerked and the

contractions spread through the places they were connected.

His cock oozed pre-come, and his balls were as hard as stones. If he didn't get inside her soon he'd blow, and he wanted to be inside her when that happened.

As he brought her down slowly from her high, he worked out how to cross the room to his nightstand for a condom without waking Lyric.

Nola lay still, her breath calming.

He planted a soft kiss to the curve of her ass, and she twitched. He grinned against her skin. "Think you can crawl into the bathroom?"

"Yes," she said unsteadily.

He pinched her bottom and she bit off a squeal. "Get goin'."

On her hands and knees she started for the bathroom, giving him an amazing glimpse of the ass he'd just tongued for the first time.

But not the last.

He followed her and closed the bathroom door most of the way, leaving only a crack in case Lyric woke up. Then he gained his feet and pulled Nola to hers too.

Her face was pink as he met her gaze. "You..."

"Were fucking fabulous? Thanks, so were you." He ran his tongue over his lips, and she flushed deeper.

He reached the top shelf and snagged a condom. With quick movements he opened it and rolled it on. "Bend over the sink, baby doll. I want you to watch yourself in the mirror when I make you come."

A shiver rolled through her. Her hair waved over her breasts, and he stripped off her nightshirt before spinning her to face the mirror. Again her ass was poised right at his cock, and damn, he wanted to take it. He nudged her back entrance with his cock. "Will you let me?"

In the mirror, her eyes were wide, the traces of sleep gone.

"I don't know if I'm ready for that yet."

He circled his hips, wanting to screw his shaft right into her. Claim her in a place no one ever had. "Okay, not today. When you're ready."

She met his gaze in the mirror and held it as he guided his erection right between the swollen walls of her pussy. She sank her teeth into her lower lip and bucked. He grabbed her hips and drew her onto tiptoe, angling deeper into her center.

His need rocketed. Her tits bounced under his assault, and he cupped them. He spread his fingers around her hard buds and pinched between his knuckles. Pleasure hooded her eyes.

"Don't close your eyes to me, baby doll. I want you to see who's fucking you." He bent his knees a little and sank a millimeter deeper.

She held his gaze in the mirror, her mouth opened on a silent gasp. Ecstasy ripped through him, starting at the base of his spine and spreading upward like wildfire in a woodland. He squeezed her nipples harder.

"Come with me. So close. So good. Sooo..." He jerked into her body, come rushing up.

She threw her head back and shuddered all over. Cream soaked him, and her pussy clamped down on him. He pumped his cock into her harder as spurts erupted from him.

What he wouldn't give to go bareback with her. The condom felt like a huge barrier between their bodies but also their souls.

As the sexual haze faded, he stared at her beautiful reflection. High color, red marks, two hickeys. Her flavors on his tongue.

She was sweet with his mother, great with Lyric. Smart, funny and amazingly talented.

He wanted her all to himself.

Forever.

He pulled free of her body and spun her into his arms. She

melted against his chest, still quivering from her release.

The notes of the song he'd written long ago rumbled from his throat.

Her muscles stiffened until she was a small sheet of board wood.

He rubbed his jaw over her bare shoulder, marking her again.

"Did Lyric's mother like that song?"

Shaking his head, he rubbed her back to calm her, just as he would a skittish animal. "That song was once for her, yes. But I soon realized it was bigger than her. She didn't deserve it. So I gave it to Lyric. But I think it's meant for someone else."

She tilted her face up to him, and he stared into the confused depths of her eyes.

"I have an urge to run to the jeweler's. Better make it quick before you go off to Nashville and find some country crooner. I want to see you in something old, something new, something borrowed and something blue. Then I want to do somethin' dirty." He quirked a brow.

She jerked from his hold and grabbed her nightshirt. Then she shoved through the bathroom door.

Lyric snuffled and started batting the air at her rude awakening.

"Nola." He followed her into the bedroom, where she was throwing on panties and jeans. Her eyes were wild.

He pointed a finger at her. "Don't you leave."

She tossed her head. "I'll go if I please. But it won't be right now. Get dressed and take care of the ranch. I've got Lyric for the day. Just don't expect me to stay tonight. I have someplace to be."

He stared at her, ignoring Lyric's grunts of anger.

She continued, "I don't belong here. I'm not your woman."

"You afraid you might like it?"

A purple stain climbed her face. She stomped past him to the sink, washed her hands then gathered Lyric out of her nest. The baby stopped fussing immediately, but Nola was far from finished.

"I don't need a husband."

"Maybe not. But I think you'd like it fine," he drawled. Suddenly making her admit how great they were together was more important than anything in the world.

"I don't want a husband," she bit off through clenched teeth. She flounced out of the bedroom with Lyric, heading for the nursery.

He trailed after her, still buck naked. "I make you feel things. Don't deny it."

"You do not." She laid Lyric on the changing table and started removing her diaper.

"You like being in my house. I see you peeking at me from the windows when I'm working outside."

Her words were constricted. "Do not!"

"And you loved when I licked you..." he lowered his voice, "...there."

She jerked her head his direction and glared at him. "Don't talk about it around Lyric. You'll corrupt her!"

He laughed, a genuine joy that washed from the pit of his stomach.

"And go get dressed, for God's sake!"

He started across the room. "You'll be in my bed tonight, Nola. Don't think about denying me," he shot over his shoulder. The last thing he saw was her eyebrows drawn low like thunderclouds over her stormy glare.

She wasn't in his bed that night.


Nola ran her palms over her glittery top and silky mini-skirt. It felt good to be dressed up and without a spit-up stain on her T-shirt. When she raised a hand to pat her hair, her bangle bracelets slid down her forearm.

The Hellion was hopping tonight. Tourists were starting to descend upon Reedy, and that meant fresh listeners. Tonight she was going to sing her own music. She'd already set it up with the guy who ran karaoke. He'd unplug for two songs, where it would be only Nola—guitar and voice.

God, she wished someone she cared about would hear her. She'd always had Molly or a friend in the crowd. Tonight she was truly solo.

Nerves zipped around her stomach like a hundred butterflies. She glanced at the big clock over the bar sporting the beer logo. She was on in two songs. Was it enough time to call Molly and get her over here?

*Forget it. I can do it alone.*

She'd been working on these songs for months. Her CDs were in Nashville even now, hopefully getting some attention. But she really needed to be there to market herself.

She shifted on her spike heels and focused on the karaoke singer. An older guy in boots and western shirt was belting out a Johnny Cash tune. The crowd cheered him on, and one woman who was young enough to be his daughter gave intermittent shrill whistles for him.

Were they a couple?

It was impossible not to think of Griffin. He was nearly twenty years older than her. In ten years, that would be them. She'd still be young and he middle-aged.

Somehow she knew he would never look like that guy onstage. Griffin would age like fine whiskey—more silver strands weaving through his beard and a few more lines on his face, but his eyes would still glitter like the youngest man's. And his physique...

Heat coiled in her core. What he'd done to her on the bedroom floor still made her blush. The memory had struck her several times throughout the day, and she'd find herself aching for more of that taboo kiss.

*Stop it.* After his mention of marriage, she'd mentally run like hell. She didn't need a proposal when she was on the cusp of fulfilling her dream of getting a record deal.

The Johnny Cash crooner took his bow to loud applause, and Nola added a few claps and a smile. Johnny Cash was always a favorite here.

A tall woman in boots and jeans took the stage. Her first note was off-key, and Nola lost interest. She stared across the crowd, picking out those she knew from high school or from around town.

"Not working at your father's office anymore?" a man leaned close to say over the caterwauling of a Carrie Underwood song.

Nola glanced at him. He was in his thirties, a cowboy-type with tobacco tucked in his cheek and a beer in hand. "Uh, no."

He raised his beer. "Can I get you a drink?"

"No, thank you. I'm up next." She gestured to the stage. The woman strutted across the short length, the spotlights showcasing her ample cleavage and the sweat glistening there.

"I always come here hoping to hear you sing."

She looked at the man harder, unsure whether to be creeped out or happy to have a fan. She tensed as he crowded into her space. Suddenly, she wanted Griffin very badly. No one would dare hit on her with him at her side.

"I'll just...go get ready," she said loud enough to be heard over the plaintive wail of the singer. She walked away from the guy, but could practically feel his gaze clinging to her ass.

Well, she'd better get used to attention, even if it was unwanted. If she became a star, she'd be lighting a spotlight on everything she did.

Still, she wanted the dream. Wanted it bad.

The singer exited the stage to a fair amount of applause, though Nola wondered if it was the audience's joy that their hearing had been saved at last.

"Nola Brady is going to step out with somethin' a little different. Give her a welcome!" the DJ intoned.

Jittery with excitement now, she circled the stage and grabbed her guitar from the case. The familiar weight of it and the pull of the strap across her shoulder felt good.

She stepped into the center of the stage, and the crowd stilled. She placed her fingers on the strings and opened her mouth. The first words that popped into her head were not her own, no matter how many times she'd rehearsed them.

Griffin's song was inside her.

She gave a little stamp of her heel and firmly shoved his voice, his words, his damn lingering touch out of her head.

The first strum of the guitar grounded her. When the words burst out, her world righted itself. For weeks she'd been off-balance, thinking about diapers and formula and long, slow kisses.

This was her—guitar, stage. She played with the audience through her song, making eye contact, dancing and swishing her ass at a sassy lyric. Cheers erupted. She no longer stood in the shade, a player on the game board of the universe. She was full of life.

Her final chord rolled into the next song—a rowdy tune about a jilted lover getting revenge. The crowd loved it.

They loved her.

Glowing from the inside out, she ended to deafening applause. Whistles and catcalls met her bow. Then she sashayed off the stage, on a high unlike any she'd known before.

This was her calling. Griffin's mention of marriage had thrown a temporary lasso around her, but she'd wriggled free and found herself again.

*Then why are those bars of his song flitting through my head?*

She shook herself and carefully placed her guitar back into her case.

"Buy ya a drink, pretty lady?" someone called to her.

She smiled and waved him off with a "thanks, anyway". Another stepped up with a fruity drink already in hand.

If Griffin were here he'd know she liked a shot glass brimming with amber liquid rather than a drink bearing an umbrella.

"No thanks. I'm driving tonight."

He looked hurt. She snagged a lady to her left and positioned the woman in front of the cowboy and his fruity drink.

"She looks thirsty," Nola said. The woman nodded, smiling wide, and the man passed the drink into her hands.

Grinning, Nola grabbed her guitar and started to push her way through the crowd.

Someone blocked her path. She looked up into the face of the man who'd spoken to her before she sang. He gave her a broad smile.

It wasn't that he wasn't attractive. He just wasn't for her.

*Admit it. No one measures up to Griffin now.*

She tossed her head to remove the thought. "Excuse me."

"Sounded beautiful, Nola. Like a dream." He leaned close. "And you look like a wet dream."

Disgust roiled in her belly. "Please move out of my way."

She could only hope the bouncer would walk her to her car. But sometimes Cliff sneaked off for a drink and a smoke with a cute girl. She cast a look around the bar for someone she knew.

The man sidled close, his beer breath fogging the air around her. He put his hand on her spine, low enough to touch her ass.

The ass Griffin had worked over until she'd lost all sense of reality.

Anger spiked in her. She didn't need Griffin's invasion. He was molding her thinking to fit his. That she belonged with him—to him.

And this guy...his family stones were about to meet the skewer of her high heel if he didn't back off.

"Get away from me. I don't welcome your advances." Her momma had raised her to be polite. Sometimes you disarmed a situation with niceness more easily than with harsh words.

The man brought his face so close to hers she practically grew drunk on his fumes. "A pretty lady like you needs a hand out. You shouldn't be carrying your guitar. Let me be your roadieee," he drawled. He leaned in, his mouth gunning for her cheek.

She jerked to the side at the last minute, but not before his sticky lips glanced off her skin. "Get off!"

Before he could do anything more, she spun and pushed her way back across the bar. People congratulated her and even asked for more songs, but she was too furious with that guy to think about singing. She wanted to put some distance between them, then she'd slip out the back door.

An old friend from high school stopped her to talk, and she spent fifteen minutes discussing people she knew and her plans to go to Nashville. All the while she talked, she kept an eye out for the stalker.

Thoughts of Griffin's warm, safe ranch filled her mind. Right now they would have made love twice and be cuddled up together under a cool sheet. He'd be seducing her into another round with those deep, chocolaty eyes and Lyric's soft sighs of sleep would be emitting through the monitor.

By the time she was done talking, Nola no longer wanted her slinky outfit or fuck-me heels. She wanted a big man's shirt and her bare toes gliding through the coarse hairs on the owner's leg.

*No. I want to go home.*

She gave the friend a hug and grabbed her guitar again, prepared to make a break for the back door. But as she started forward, the crowd parted and she got a clear shot of the stalker standing against the wall where she'd have to pass to get to the back door.

"Fuck."

She whirled and headed in the opposite direction, making a beeline for the front exit. People moved aside for her, and if they didn't a little nudge with her guitar case did the trick.

She burst out into the cool night air, relief coursing through her veins. She settled her gaze on her car and quickened her step.

A crunch of boots on gravel behind her raised hairs all over her body. It was him. She knew it.

*Don't look back. Just get to the car.* She delved a hand into her neckline, located her car keys stuffed safely in her bra and pulled them free. Holding the jagged metal between the knuckles of her first two fingers made her feel slightly more in control. If he came at her, she'd strike with the sharp key. Hopefully that would buy her enough time to get to her car.

The steps behind her grew faster, closer. Her breathing hitched in her lungs. Forty more paces to the car. Why, oh why had she parked this far away?

Actually, she didn't have a choice. When she'd arrived, the lot had been packed.

"Where's the fire, little lady? Oh yeah, in my pants."

The door of The Hellion opened again, and music pulsed out. Nola shot a glance over her shoulder, praying the person who'd exited would act as a buffer between her and the stalker.

Part of her mind dipped low, thinking this was all her fault—that she shouldn't have paraded herself in front of all those people. She'd only been asking for something like this to happen.

Then she got angry. No, she wasn't at fault. This guy needed to be put in his place.

"Stay away from me," she called out in a voice firmer than she felt inside.

A truck bounced into the parking lot, headlights washing over her. Then the engine revved, and the tires spun gravel as the driver stepped on the gas.

She took off toward her car, cursing her heels on the uneven ground. Her heart thrummed, a trapped bird with the chance at freedom. Her guitar thumped her outer thigh.

"Hey, you crazy sonofabitch!" the stalker hollered.

The truck braked in a spray of gravel, and Nola reached her car as the driver got out. Big shoulders passed before his headlights as he went after her stalker.

"You bugging this woman?"

The voice sliced through Nola.

Griffin. She dropped her guitar and watched him make a lunge at the stalker. How the hell had he found out? Had he been parked in the dark, watching her escape?

The stalker danced back a few steps and said something she couldn't hear. Griffin strode forward, his body rolling like a predator's. She shivered and wrapped her arms around her middle.

"What did you say?" Griffin barked.

This time she heard the stalker loud and clear. "You her daddy?"

"That's what I thought you said." Griffin threw himself forward. He and the stalker landed in a pile of thrashing limbs and angry words.

Shaking, Nola ran to them. Headlights glared over their bodies. The stalker threw a punch, and Griffin caught his fist. A quick twist made the man howl and fall back, grunting in pain.

Griffin climbed to his feet and glared down at him. "Better wander back inside and call 911. I'm pretty sure you just dislocated your elbow."

"Motherfucker!"

Nola made a sound, and Griffin looked right at her. In the ring of light, he appeared to be an avenging angel. "You okay?"

"Y-yes."

"Get your guitar and get in my truck."

His command sent a heated thrill right to her pussy, but her heart bucked in disobedience.

"No, I can make it home now."

"Don't make me put you in my truck, Nola. Get. In." When she didn't budge, he pressed his lips together and his shoulders sagged. "Please?"

She passed a shaky hand over her face then nodded. She wouldn't go home with him, wouldn't fall into his arms again. They had to break off this insane love affair before she was mired too deep to follow her dreams.

He watched her as she gathered her guitar, standing sentry over the man writhing on the ground. When Nola neared, Griffin took the guitar from her and placed it in the back of his truck. Then he opened the passenger's door and gestured for her to get in.

She did, barely making the climb in her heels and short skirt. At her struggle, he gripped her hips and boosted her in. She bounced and locked her knees together, her arms around her chest.

Griffin got in too and closed them inside the truck. Silence was a thousand pounds of concrete on her chest, smothering her.

"How'd you find out?" she squeaked.

His angry glare might be for her or the residue of his fury with the stalker. "Rick saw the guy hassling you and called me."

"How'd you get here so fast?"

"You're not the only one who can make it from Needle's Pass to Reedy in twenty minutes."

Damn, she was linked too tightly to Griffin already. People were starting to connect them in their minds.

Her shaking started in earnest. Griffin plucked her into his arms and deposited her on his lap. She tried to scramble off. His touch would be her undoing—tears threatened.

"Goddammit, woman. Don't you see you're in shock? Do you think a little country gal like you is scared half out of her wits every day?"

His words infuriated her. He made her seem like some dim-witted young girl, unable to handle herself.

*What would I have done? That guy's a hundred pounds heavier. He could toss me over his shoulder like a hay bale.*

Her stomach bottomed out, making her glad she hadn't drunk anything.

Griffin flexed his arms around her, bringing her nose against his soft flannel shirt. His piney scent and warmth almost stole her control. He felt so right. And he'd hurt a man to keep her safe.

Maybe she was an innocent, cut from the bolt of country cloth that would act as a net for her, keeping her from being savvy enough to survive in any other environment.

Like Nashville.

She swallowed hard and pushed away from Griffin's chest. He let her move but kept his arms wreathed loosely around her back.

"Come home with me," he said hoarsely.

She drowned in his dark tones and all they implied. Shaking her head, she said, "No."

"Let me take you home then."

She couldn't sit in the same vehicle with him and not want his lips on every inch of her body. She shook her head again. "I'll drive myself. Go home, Griffin."

He twisted his gaze from hers. She nearly buckled at the hurt etched across his handsome features. The errant lock of hair that always fell into his eyes drooped, and she clenched her fingers to keep from brushing it away.

She reached for the door handle. He released her, and she climbed out. He didn't move to help her down though her legs were obviously trembling. She glanced at the ground in front of the headlights. The stalker must have crawled off while she sat in Griffin's arms.

Nola retrieved her guitar and made it back to her car before her tears broke loose. The dam shoring up her self-doubt crumbled. She slid behind the wheel and let the drops trickle down her face.

Only when she backed out did Griffin drive away too, headed in the other direction, up to Needle's Pass.

She couldn't keep her thoughts from touching on his ma, who been picked up at the hospital and been set up in the guest room again. He'd probably awakened her to sit with Lyric so Griffin could come and save the day.

His words dug into Nola's psyche. She was all country, had only ever visited a handful of cities. Her family vacationed in the mountains in a tent, not in New York City. She'd been sheltered from dangers, living all of her years under her parents' roof. She'd never dealt with a belligerent neighbor or even an irate customer.

By the time she rolled into her driveway, she felt so low. Disheartened.

Molly opened the door for her after she knocked five times. "Where the hell's your key?"

"Couldn't fit it in my bra." She straggled past her sister, guitar in hand.

Molly shut the door and spun on her. The woman wore only a camisole and a scrap of lace for panties, always ready for action that had yet to come. "Can't fit a whole hell of a lot in that outfit."

"You're one to talk." Nola set down her guitar, annoyance instantly roused.

"You have a good time tonight?"

"Not so much," Nola said softly.

"That man of yours show up to hear you sing?"

"No..." He showed up for other reasons. Maybe the most important reasons.

"I knew it," Molly said. "You finally drove him away, didn't you? Don't you realize a man like that only comes into your life once? You let him go and you're left with drunks, cheaters, liars, lazy asses. You're throwing away something great—"

"Shut. Up." Nola glared at her sister. Too well she realized she might be making the error of her life, but she couldn't very well tow him, his sick ma and Lyric across the country to reach her dream of becoming a country singer. Even hauling them in her mind would be too much baggage.

After tonight, she felt so close to that goal. The crowd loved her—her songs.

Griffin's low voice revolved around her head all of a sudden. *Only one lyric important enough to sing to you.*

"I'm going into the studio."

"Make sure you don't wake us again," Molly spat and strode away.

Nola stifled a growl and took her guitar into the basement studio. She only lit one lamp and sat in the golden ring of light, a meager spotlight where she sang not her own song, but Griffin's.

# Chapter Ten

"You doin' all right, Ma?" Griffin held her elbow and guided her out of the sedan his mother drove before she got sick. She was still far from her normal, hardy self but today she seemed less fragile.

"Yeah, yeah. Stop coddling me." She waved but wore a smile. From the backseat where her car seat was secured, Lyric squawked, ready to get out too.

"Just a second, sweetheart." He made eye contact with her, and she flapped.

Dragging Lyric to the hospital for chemotherapy and blood work wasn't ideal, but he was faring. Just as he was making it work to have her in the barn. He strapped her into the bouncy chair and put it somewhere safe while he worked. She didn't mind watching him shovel or feed animals. And she often stared at the birds flitting through the rafters.

But this wouldn't work forever. His daughter's feet were already hanging off the edge of the seat. Another month and she also wouldn't put up with not being mobile. Since the night she'd rolled off the bed, she'd begun to roll all over the place. He'd put her on a blanket on the living room floor and a few minutes later find her in the kitchen.

And fuck, he missed Nola's presence in his bed.

She'd done so much for him around the house. Just having a break from folding miniature laundry or mixing formula had been welcomed.

But he missed her in the way a man did a woman, with a bone-deep need. To hear her voice, listen to her singing. Feel her wrapped around every damn inch of him.

His ma waited on the sidewalk while he snagged the baby seat from the car. His chest was tight. Today his mother would find out whether or not the cancer had stalled enough to operate.

She still faced a radical mastectomy, but they could deal with that.

The doctor's office was jam-packed. He let his ma take the only available seat and leaned against the wall, Lyric in her seat at his feet. She blinked up at him and he pulled a face that made her give a drooly grin.

Glancing up, he caught a woman smiling at him. Around his age with a wide-eyed beauty. She sat beside a woman who was probably her mother.

He looked her over more closely. She was in the same stage of life as he was. He stole a look at her bare ring finger. Perhaps she was divorced with kids and also bearing the responsibility of a loved one's illness. He could smile at her and start a conversation. Take her to dinner.

But he wasn't looking for a companion. One had just fallen into his lap when Nola took the nanny job.

He gave the woman a little nod. Then Lyric started churning her arms and legs, gearing up to scream, he bent and unbuckled her, pulling her free. He straightened with her hooked in his arm, facing forward so she could look around.

The woman across the space smiled wider. "She's beautiful."

"Thank you." He jiggled Lyric a bit, more out of nervousness than because she fussed. He didn't want to get to know anyone but a little country singer with a spitfire attitude and the voice of an angel.

She was headed to Nashville soon. It had been a week since the night he raced to her at The Hellion, but a few well-timed questions at the drugstore about the family had let him know she hadn't left yet.

The nurse opened the door to the waiting room and called a name. The woman he'd spoken to stood and helped her mother to her feet. They made their way into the office.

He felt his shoulders droop in relief. Lyric made a few angry noises, so he plugged her mouth with a finger. She gnawed on him for a bit. Drool slid down the back of his hand.

His ma was engrossed in a health magazine, reading with her glasses pushed down her nose. She wore a simple, chic scarf around her head today. The red color flattered her and made her look almost okay.

Almost.

He pressed his lips into a line. Things had to go right for him at this appointment. If they learned his ma wasn't well enough for the surgery, he didn't know how he'd react. Maybe he'd twist the doctor's arm and dislocate his elbow too.

His ire rushed up fast and hard, like a river swelling after a heavy rain. That weasel of a man at The Hellion had asked if Griffin was Nola's father.

Over the past week, he'd played and replayed that through his mind. Did they truly look so mismatched? When he glimpsed their reflections in the mirror together, he saw only perfection. He ignored the silver strands in his beard or the fact he'd been losing his virginity when she'd been wetting her pants.

Age hadn't mattered when he was buried inside her, their gazes locked as they made love. Fell in love.

He was sure he wasn't the only one to feel it. The glow in her eyes was only there for him.

His ma rustled the pages of the magazine, and Lyric was ready for a new chew toy. He removed his finger from her mouth and bent to dig through the diaper bag for her favorite teething ring. She batted it aside and issued a shriek.

The entire office looked at him, and he gave a smile of apology. Bending to his mother's ear, he said, "I'll just take her out for a minute, Ma."

"I'll be fine."

He was glad to hear that old spark of independence in his mother. As he made his way outside with Lyric, his mind returned to Nola. He was like a dog with a bone. He couldn't stop digging it up.

Strolling down the sidewalk, he showed Lyric the pink flowers in the bushes. One fat fist closed around a bloom and she plucked it off, directing it to her mouth. He pulled it free before she did more than touch her lips with it.

He pivoted on the sidewalk and headed back up. The town of Reedy was laid out before him. Small side streets and quaint buildings. Houses close together. One of them was the Brady residence. He could probably find it with his eyes shut. In the week since they'd been apart, he'd traced and retraced the route to it.

Maybe she'd be open to him paying her a visit. He could take his ma home and drive back. When Nola opened the door, he'd rip her off her feet and claim her mouth. Letting her know just where she belonged.

With a shake of his head, he paced in the opposite direction again. He let Lyric pull off another flower. This time she marveled at it, holding it in front of her face and not trying to eat it.

There was a florist's shop on the main street. What he wouldn't give for extra cash to buy Nola a bouquet. Woo her a little. Not middle-aged rancher style but proper boyfriend.

Lyric aimed the flower at her mouth, and he removed it from her hand. Then he held her up in front of him. "Let's see if it's time for Nana's appointment."

His daughter gave him a toothless grin. They headed inside just as the nurse called for Alice Turner.

For the next half hour he listened to the doctor speak about chances and percentages. But by the time they walked out, he felt the first stirrings of hope.

"You all right about this surgery being scheduled for next week?" he asked his ma once they were in the car again.

"I don't see how I have a choice." She sat in the backseat, holding a bottle for Lyric. The baby's snorting noises as she sucked filled the space.

"No, but it's good news. We're kicking the cancer's ass." He glanced at her before turning out of town for the road leading to Needle's Pass.

"I relish the thought." His ma's voice was more like her familiar tone.

He grinned. "What do you think about spending the afternoon alone? You'll be okay?"

"Sure." She stared at his profile until he swung his head to look at her. "You thinking of taking a trip?"

"Yes. Lyric and I want to visit an old friend."

His ma made a noise. "Lyric's been missing that friend, I think."

The corner of his mouth twitched up. Excitement wove through him at the idea of driving back to Reedy and setting eyes on the beautiful woman who haunted him.

His smile spread over his mouth and up to his eyes. He nodded. "Been thinkin' that myself."


Nola held the long note on her song, rippling through the octave. For a week she'd been working hard at her music. Writing poetry and putting the words to music. She'd played guitar until her fingertips burned and sang until she grew hoarse.

It felt good.

She was almost ready to go. She'd book the flight today.

Pausing in her song, she grabbed the pen and scribbled out a word on her page. Then she wrote in a new word.

The faint notes of the doorbell sounded above. She blew out a breath and set aside her guitar. By the time she ran the flight of stairs and got to the front door, the doorbell had rung four times.

"What's so important?" she asked as she threw open the door.

Her heart convulsed, and her pussy clenched at the sight of the big man filling her doorway. T-shirt straining perfectly over his broad chest and sleeves bulging around biceps that had supported him while he moved within Nola.

And Lyric rode on his arm, bright eyes centering on Nola in recognition.

"This is what's so important." He stepped into the house, crowding her back. Then he hooked one arm around her and crashed his mouth over hers.

She sucked in a breath, filling her nose with his piney, musky scent she'd spent a damn week craving. She'd gone through her duffle bag twice, smelling articles of clothing for a hint of the man she'd stayed with.

He swept her mouth with his tongue. A quiet mewl burst from her as the chorus to his song played through her head.

He lifted his head. She stared up at him for a long heartbeat. Rattled. More turned-on than ever, and rapidly forgetting her decision to stay away from Griffin and head straight to Nashville.

That flight seemed destined for someone else. She belonged here, pressed against him, with Lyric's chubby hand moving over her hair.

The baby yanked, and Griffin huffed with laughter. "Now, Lyric, that's no way to greet our friend."

If he'd said *my lover* she would have whirled away and run for the phone to book that flight. But his use of friend made her pause.

Countless hours they'd spent lying in bed talking, his callused fingers playing over her skin while she related her favorite color, what subjects she'd excelled at in school. And how she liked to use a certain note in her voice to hook the crowd.

And he'd told her things too. His best subjects in school had been math and science. His favorite color was red because she looked gorgeous in it, and he had a thing for tanned legs in cowgirl boots.

He'd also talked at length with her about the operations on the ranch. She'd never imagined she'd be interested in such things, but she'd hung on his every low-pitched word.

She and Griffin were friends.

And her pussy throbbed for him.

"Why are you here?" she asked, trying to vanquish the breathy tone from her voice.

His dark eyes burned, riveting her to the floor. She couldn't move to make a call if the house were on fire. "What can I do to make you come back?"

His gritty words shot down any argument she might have raised. Warmth bloomed low in her belly, even when Lyric tugged hard at her hair.

She missed him, missed the baby. She wanted to make Alice hot tea when she woke up, and she wanted to sleep with her head on Griffin's muscled chest.

She swayed toward him, and he caught her, tucking her so tightly against him she couldn't move, and didn't want to anyway. Tilting her face up to his, she hooked her arm around his neck. The soft curls on his nape tickled her bare skin.

"Teach me that damn song, Griffin. I can't get it out of my head."

He dropped his forehead to hers, staring into her eyes up close. Nola laid a palm on Lyric's rounded belly and felt the child's heart fluttering under her fingertips as her father's heart thrummed against her breasts.

"Get your things, baby doll. There's only one place I can properly teach that song."

She swallowed hard at the heat in his gaze. "Where's that?"

"My bed."

# Chapter Eleven

Griffin nuzzled the sweetly scented backside of Nola's knee. She squirmed, but he tightened the circle of his fingers around her ankle. "It comes only once."

He snaked his tongue over her skin, and she echoed the line with a squeak. He smiled and dragged his teeth lightly down to her calf. Her head was turned sharply in the covers, face flushed pink.

"Ah, c'mon, country singer. You can do better than that," he chided, sucking on the tight swell of her calf.

Seeing her curled toes did more to his ego than anything in his life. He worked his way down to her ankle as she repeated the lyric again, this time in a clearer voice.

"Beautiful," he murmured against her skin, and pressed a trail of kisses up to her thigh. He moved to her inner thigh. She parted her legs and raised her ass to present her dripping-wet pussy.

The folds glistened with the cream of two orgasms he'd given—with his mouth then fingers. But it wasn't enough. When she left his bed this time, she'd be so thoroughly loved, she'd be ruined for another man.

Even in Nashville, she'd touch herself while thinking of him.

He slithered his tongue right into her wet folds. She cried out and bucked. For long minutes he tongue-fucked her before lifting his head. "Sing it to me, baby doll. All of it."

She rocked her hips and slipped a hand between the mattress and her body, going right for her clit.

He caught her hand and stopped her. "My pussy. You release for me. Now sing."

Breathing hard, she collapsed against the bed and sang his song in such a sweet voice, tears jumped into his eyes.

God, didn't she see how right she was for him? How well they worked and played together?

A voice in the back of his mind said she needed to fulfill her dreams. And he'd let her. Right after she wore his goddamn ring.

When she finished the song verse, he released her hand and flipped her over. She stretched before him, golden flesh and strawberry-blonde waves. Her eyes were hazy with passion and her lips swollen from sucking his cock.

He still hadn't penetrated her. They weren't to that part of the song yet.

She reached for him. When her short nails grazed his shoulders, his cock lengthened another fraction. He gained his knees and angled it right at her pussy. The damn condom he'd been wearing for several minutes felt like a constricting band.

He tunneled against her pussy lips, parting them around his aching head. The next verse of the song came out gritty. She hooked a leg around his hip and tugged him hard, but he resisted her.

A frustrated noise erupted from her throat, but her eyes were soft. "I'll run through the rain for you. Only one lyric important enough to sing to you..."

Jeezus. Did that mean...? Was she admitting it?

He thrust home. His cock buried to the root in her tight, hot pussy. "I love you," he rasped the next lyric, and began to move.

She wrapped her other leg around him and rose and fell with the tempest of their lovemaking. When he found her lips, she delivered an emotion-packed kiss that drove all the worries from his mind.

With her by him, he could face anything. Ten surgeries with Ma and Lyric's mouthy years. He could survive another calving season like the one he'd just had, losing all the calves to sickness again.

She swirled her hips against his, and the head of his cock ground against her deepest point. He growled and bit into her lower lip. She panted the same line. "Only one lyric...important enough...Fuck, Griffin! Make me come!"

He withdrew, gripped her ass to get a better angle and pounded into her. The orgasm rushed over him, and their flesh slapped in a wild tune. Her inner walls gripped him perfectly, clenching and releasing in rapid succession as he poured into her body.

Then he captured her mouth again and poured all his emotion into that caress. Their breathing slowed. She ran her hands over his spine. Each pass felt like love.

Though she hadn't stated it.

He rolled them until she lay atop him. Her weight aroused him all over again, and his cock twitched inside her.

She giggled. "Already? It's been thirteen seconds."

"Thirteen seconds too long."

She pressed a noisy kiss on his pec, sucking the skin until it burned, and he knew she'd left a mark. He wanted to roar with satisfaction.

"Tell me something good about your week, Griffin."

He didn't even hesitate. "When you opened the door to me."

A quiet noise left her, and her gaze melted further. "Something else."

"Finding out Ma is ready for the surgery. I'm eager to get to the next stage of this fight."

She nodded, suddenly sober. "It's great news."

"Yeah, the tumor growth has stopped enough to operate."

"When is the surgery?" she asked.

He scuffed his beard over her shoulder until she shivered. "Next week."

She fell still. "What will you do with Lyric?"

He met her real question head-on. "Yes, I need you here. Will you stay?"

Part of him knew how selfish he was being, keeping her from the pursuit of her music career, but he couldn't exactly keep Lyric happy in a hospital waiting room for hours. Then what would he do while he visited his ma in recovery? He needed help, and Nola could save his ass.

And keep him from going crazy with worry too.

She searched his gaze. Then slowly nodded. "I'll stay."

Joy flitted through his system. He ran his hands over her arms and threaded their fingers. "I have another important question for you."

Her throat worked around a swallow. "What's that?"

He tightened his ab muscles and leaned up to bite her tender earlobe. "Will you shower with me?"

She ground her pussy against his erection, which had slipped from her body. "Only if you promise to wear a condom."

"Hell," he breathed, "yes."

He led her to the bathroom and started the shower. Beyond the narrow window, the ranch slumbered. Inside the house, his daughter slept. And he'd go to the barn tomorrow bleary-eyed with lack of sleep. But damn if he would stop loving her all night long.

He crowded her into the shower and pinned her to the wall. Her wet length ignited him, and he used his chin to brush aside damp tendrils of her hair so he could get at her throat.

"No marks, Griffin. They just went away."

"That's why I want to put them back," he groaned, opening his mouth over her flesh.

147

She twisted in his hold, bringing her wet breasts against his chest. "I mean it. No marks. I feel like a sixteen-year-old hiding them from my parents."

"Don't hide 'em." He went after her again.

Sagging at the knees, she slipped from his clutches. "I'll give you something else, Griffin."

He let his gaze lazily over her. Full breasts, toned belly, a faint patch of gold-red curls on her mound, and round, delicious thighs. "Damn right you are."

"What about..." She turned and braced her hands against the wall, thrusting her ass into the air. "This?"

He stopped breathing.


Nola's inner thigh muscles quivered at the thought of what she was about to do. Before Griffin had entered her life, she'd never contemplated anal sex. But he awakened things in her.

He soaped his hands and ran them down her sides. Bubbles formed on her skin, which he lathered into a white foam. When he ran his big palms around to cup her breasts, she sagged against the wall.

He nuzzled her throat, and her skin pebbled at the touch of his beard. "You're sure, baby doll? I don't want to push you."

In response she shoved her ass against his erection. He groaned.

"Give me two minutes."

"Make it one."

He climbed out of the shower, and a minute later appeared with a white tube and his cock stretched inside a tight condom. He scanned her face. "Keep licking your lips and this won't last even one."

She reached for him, but he spun her to face the wall again. Then he took his time lathering her clit. Tendrils of heat climbed her core. The knot inside her tightened, and she almost begged for him to give her release.

Clamping down on her urges, she let him take the reins. He was the cowboy, after all.

He glided his finger over her straining nubbin down through her slick folds. He eased a fingertip into her pussy, and she bucked. At the same moment, his other hand found a different opening.

He circled her anus with a rough finger. Once...twice. Then plunged right into her. She cried out at the invasion. The well-lubed finger gave nothing but pleasure. She rocked, and he withdrew only to plunge again.

"I'm gonna stretch you for me. When you can take two fingers, maybe three, I'll put this in you." He nudged her hip with his thick erection.

She reached behind her and gripped his nape. She twisted her head for a kiss, and he explored her mouth until her knees threatened to buckle. He thrust his tongue in and out in time with the finger in her ass.

When her body started clenching around him on the exit, he growled. The next blissful stab was two fingers.

She muffled a cry against her forearm. The pleasure pain of his addition whipped through her. She lost herself for several breath-holding minutes as he worked over her ass.

Nashville had never seemed so far away. She was locked into this moment. Here with Griffin.

The rasp of his breath against her neck spoke of how turned on he was. Power welled within her, very close to what she felt onstage. She had the ability to command an audience—had known it since a very young age. And now she was learning she could do that with a man too.

Not just anyone though. Griffin was different.

As he withdrew his fingers, her heart dropped into her belly.

*I'm so screwed. I love him.*

The situation was less than fairy tale, yet here she stood, wanting him to do everything to her and in every possible way, just so she could carry away the memory when she left.

Dark need tore through her.

"Three fingers," she gasped.

He hesitated, flicking her clit until juices oozed from her pussy.

"I'm so close," she whispered.

"I know, doll." He pressed on her nether hole again, and she shoved back for more.

Three fingers entered her, swift and easy.

"Holy. Fuck. You're like a glove. Once I slide into that tight hole, I'm not gonna last. I shoulda jacked off before getting in the shower." His voice was a mix of mirth and regret.

Her laughter filled the shower, and her arousal spiked. Reaching behind her, she located his swollen shaft. She pumped it slowly. With a groan, he jerked his hips back.

"What do you want?" His voice at her ear raised a shiver.

"You. Right where your fingers were."

"Here?" He covered her pulsing button with a forefinger. Fresh cream squeezed from her.

She shook her head, and water from her hair sprayed the wall. "You know where."

"You're right. But I want to hear you say it."

"Say...?"

He tugged her earlobe with his teeth and ground her clit into her body again. "Say, 'Griffin, fill my ass with your cock'." He teased her back opening with one lubed finger.

"One isn't enough anymore." Nola's voice sounded whiney, and he laughed.

"Then say it."

She smeared water from her eyes with her forearm. She'd never known abandon in the bedroom like she did with him. Maybe it was his experience or his confidence. Now he was luring her confidence to the surface too.

A determination to match him in all ways—kiss for kiss, thrust for thrust—rose inside her.

And she would damn well best him with dirty words.

"Baby, drive your thick cock into my ass and let me milk it dry."

He went still, his fingers fumbling to a halt on her clit.

Her mind flew over what she'd just said. Why wasn't he reacting? Why—

"That was better than I could have dreamed of, baby doll." He tapped her clit and pushed his cock against her opening. She spread around him with surprising ease.

The feeling of his well-lubed shaft sliding into her stole all thought. The pressure consumed her, and she wanted more.

"Relax," he crooned in her ear, though his words sounded tight. "Open for me."

She sagged, and he wrapped an arm around her middle for support. Then he drooped at the knees and slid in another inch. She sucked in a harsh breath.

"Fucking hell. Shit. Goddamn." His torrent of curses could only mean one thing—his need matched hers.

She arched her lower back and took another inch.

"Oh my... Damn, baby doll. You're strangling my cock with your tight ass." She opened her mouth to apologize, but he said, "I can't get enough. I need it all."

With one solid shove, he rooted himself deep in her body. She cried out as heat rolled through her and her inner walls clamped down on him.

"Sonofabitch," he growled and began to move.

Every pass of his thick erection through her body rocketed

her toward the peak. Her clit throbbed in time to her heart. Just a few strokes of a finger would get her off, but something so much bigger built inside her.

He gripped her hips and pulled her down on his shaft. "You can't fucking believe how gorgeous this looks, my cock disappearing into your round ass. Motherfuck."

She smiled at his cussing though her body began to tense with a brand new pressure. Deep in her core, a pulsation began.

Griffin groaned, and she issued a small squeak. "Tell me you're going to come. Tell me."

"I'm...going to die if you don't move faster."

"Fucking sweet hell!" He pumped in a frenzied rhythm and reached between her legs again. The first swipe of her clit tipped her over the ledge.

She freefell, mind floating, body thrumming with ecstasy. Her ass clenched and released around him, and her pussy flooded.

He angled lower and gained another fraction of an inch at the same moment she felt his liquid heat fill her. He managed to bite off a roar of satisfaction, but she felt it rumble from his chest into her back, vibrating to every corner of her body.

And soul.

*Oh God.*

"Tell me," he rasped.

Confusion swept her until she realized he wasn't finished speaking.

"Tell me you'll marry me, baby doll."

If he'd asked her to talk dirtier, to go down on her knees and pull off his condom and suck his cock, she would have.

But she couldn't do what he asked.

When he pulled free of her body, she felt an aching loss. Tears sprang to her eyes. He spun her to face him. She wouldn't meet his gaze, and he used his knuckles under her chin to meet her eyes.

"Hear that?" His eyes took on a faraway expression. Through her haze of passion and emotion, she fought to follow his question.

"No," she murmured.

"It's raining. Hear it on the roof?"

She let her gaze wander over his beautiful face. Rugged features, dark hair, blazing eyes. She could have him if she wanted. As a child she'd dreamed of riding a horse to her wedding rather than walking down the aisle. She'd told Molly once, and her sister had latched on with fervor.

Images flipped through Nola's mind, snapshots of what could be. Something old? Her family's heirloom veil. New—a sexy lace thong. Molly would let her borrow her trademark red lipstick, and for something blue...maybe they'd dress Lyric in a pretty blue tutu.

*Oh fuck, I'm never getting to Nashville.*

Griffin's dark gaze threatened to break her. She sucked back a sob, but he smiled. Turning off the water, he said, "Come on."

He tugged her out of the shower. She reached for a plush towel on the shelf, but he stopped her. "Don't dry off. We're about to get wetter." He rolled off the condom and disposed of it. Then gave his hands a cursory wash before grabbing her hand and towing her out of the bathroom.

When they reached his bedroom door, she balked. "We can't go out there naked."

"Why not? It's my house."

"Someone might see us," she hissed.

His eyes crinkled. "No one is within a country mile. C'mon, baby doll."

Her heart pattered a staccato like the rain on the roof. It

was really coming down. She hoped it was warm, because she didn't relish standing nude in a cold downpour.

Her gaze fell over Griffin's sculpted backside and heat spread through her. He'd keep her warm.

They traipsed through the dark rooms to the mudroom. She expected him to grab the old black umbrella in the corner, but he ignored it and dragged her right out into the yard.

The muggy night surrounded her like a lover's embrace. Fat droplets bounced off her face, her breasts. The warm sting exhilarated her, and she tipped her face to the sky.

When she dropped her chin, she found Griffin's stare on her. She fell into his arms. He caught her waist and her hand to whirl her. Her bare feet sank into the soggy grass, and his hard body stuck to hers.

He spun her all over the yard. They tripped over a chair leg, and he narrowly righted them before they sprawled to the ground. That spurred her giggles, and he followed. They shook with laughter, and tears of joy and sadness ran free with the rain washing over her face.

The wind kicked up, throwing more water at them, but he just scooped her up and danced on. They'd danced the first time they'd met at The Hellion. And she'd been smitten then.

Now she was positively lost.

Their gazes clashed like lightning, and Griffin swooped in to claim her mouth. His strong arms circling her and the drum of his heart against her breasts only added to the moment. He slipped his tongue against hers in a long, slow kiss that packed more emotional punch than a romantic comedy.

She quivered. If he raised his head and asked her to marry him again, she didn't have the strength to go on fighting it. She'd get that whole list of somethings that came with a wedding, including the "somethin' dirty" he'd promised her before.

He swirled his tongue through her mouth in a new dance. She sighed and locked her arms around his neck. They swayed together for long, drenching moments.

Finally he raised his head and stared right into her eyes.

But he didn't ask again.

# Chapter Twelve

At the sound of tires on gravel, Griffin leaned the shovel against the fence and walked around the barn to see the drive. After two days of drenching rain, the ranch was a sopping mess of mud. The animals had torn up the pastures right quick, and the downspout on the house wasn't draining properly. A small pool stood at the corner.

If Lyric were a year or two older, she'd be sitting in it. A swimming pool for a country girl.

He smiled at his thoughts and at the sight of Taylor getting out of his truck. He wore a black slicker, which flapped in the wind. Griffin hollered his name, and Taylor raised a hand in greeting.

By the time Taylor reached him, his friend's hat was soaked. Griffin led the way to the barn. The comfort of clean hay and animal enveloped him. Nothing like a warm, dry place to rest and bullshit with a friend.

Taylor clapped him on the back. "Nasty day to help on the ranch."

"Yeah, well, I was about to stop anyway. Can't do much in this mud."

Taylor leaned against a stall and looked in at Bart, the old horse Griffin had been nursing year after year of life. "This the horse you got right after high school?"

"Yeah, he's about to go to the permanent pasture in the sky, but I can't bring myself to put him down. Not when he's still happy to see me." Griffin leaned against the door too and patted Bart's nose. The chestnut horse flicked his tail.

Silence stretched between them, only broken by the constant beat of rain. Days of rain seemed to affect some people's moods, but not Griffin's.

Nola had taken one look at the window and put her head back under the covers. But then Lyric's coos had transmitted through the monitor, and Nola tossed back the blankets to Griffin's laughter. In the end, Griffin had tended his daughter. Changing, dressing and feeding her was bonding time he'd never give up.

After a spell, Taylor said, "You sure you wanna do this, man?"

Griffin gave a short nod. "Yeah. Got no choice."

"You know what you're giving up, right?"

Sighing, Griffin thought about selling the old 1948 Indian Chief motorcycle. His grandfather had purchased it after WWII, kept it in pristine condition and passed it to his grandson. There was a time when Griffin could have gotten any girl he wanted with that bike.

Now he was giving it up because he wanted a woman.

Taylor glanced at him. "If you want to back out, just say the word."

"No, I need to sell. I'd rather the bike be with someone I know and trust will take care of it."

"You know if you need money, I can spot you some."

Griffin's chest tightened at the offer. No one knew better what kind of strain he was under than Taylor. No new calves to take to market, massive tuition bill still unpaid, and keeping Nola just got more expensive. He planned to buy her a ring.

He gripped Taylor's shoulder and squeezed. "Appreciate that. But no, I'll sell the bike. It's best all around."

Taylor shifted, his boots scuffing the worn floorboards. "If you ever want it back..."

"All I'll have to do is come up with the cash, I know. C'mon,

Em Petrova

let's load it up." Griffin strode from the barn and through the rain to the shed where he kept the bike. Taylor ducked into the space as Griffin switched on the light.

The prized motorcycle sat in the middle of the room under a tarp. Griffin hurried through removing the tarp. Every polished inch spoke of the care he'd continued to heap upon the bike.

Taylor blew out a whistle. "This is gonna finally get me a little hottie."

Griffin eyed him. "Oh, it will get you a lot of little hotties. But they won't be the right kind of women. You know that."

"I do, but damn, I'm gonna have a good time being reminded."

Griffin snorted with laughter.

"Your country singer sure would look pretty on the back of this bike." The seat didn't really accommodate a second rider, but Griffin had made it work more times than he could count in his youth.

Stomach warming at talk of Nola, Griffin gave a noncommittal nod.

Taylor pushed on. "Just exactly what do you plan to do with the money?"

"Pay Miranda's bills."

"There will be plenty of cash left."

"Gonna buy a few more horses at auction."

"Thinking of phasing out Angus beef?"

Griffin ran a hand over the smooth leather bike seat. "No, just supplement. Raise some prime stock to sell. Always a market for horses."

"That's true." Taylor gave him a sidelong look. "You're gonna buy her a ring, aren't you?"

A long, slow breath expelled from Griffin. The magnitude of what he was about to do hit him. It scared the living shit out of

158

him, actually. Especially since he'd asked her twice and she'd responded by telling him she was leaving for Nashville, then by saying nothing at all. Odds were he'd be stuck with a diamond ring when all was said and done.

"I don't have a choice, Taylor. I'm in love with her."

Taylor shot him a crooked grin. "I can see that, man. Think she'll say yes?"

"No." Griffin's word sounded final even to him. He spun away to grab the helmet from the hook on the wall. When he voiced his worst fears, his voice cracked. "I think she'll refuse me and hightail it outta here, straight for Nashville. But it's the risk I have to take."

"You can go to Nashville with her."

Griffin met his gaze head-on. "Give up the ranch, move away from Ma during the years she'll most need me? Besides, I'm only qualified to shovel shit and care for hooves. I don't know anything about city life."

"Neither does Nola. She's lived here all her life."

"That's true. Listen, are you takin' this bike today or not?"

Taylor, as stoic as always, rolled with Griffin's change of topic. "Sure am. I'll get the truck and pull it around."

Griffin helped him load the heirloom bike into the back of the truck. And as he accepted a personal check for half of his yearly income, he swallowed down the feeling he was about to make the biggest mistake of his life. But as he'd told Taylor, he didn't have a choice. His heart was urging him on like a rider hell-bent for the finish line and the golden cup.

As Nola drifted down the sidewalk, she jostled her purse to her other arm. It was a change of pace to be out on her own and without a sixteen-pound baby in her arms. For once Nola had on nice clothes and her hair was freshly styled from a salon

159

Em Petrova

visit.

Griffin had insisted upon sending Nola away for a much-needed day off, saying it was about time he and Lyric had some daddy-daughter time. But Nola felt a little despondent at being sent away.

Since coming back, she hadn't felt chained down to a job. No, she was looking at the situation in a whole new light, which was terrifying.

The lyrics to Griffin's song revolved through her mind, on a constant loop. For weeks she'd eaten, drank, heard nothing but those words. *Only one lyric important enough to sing to you. Ain't nothin' gonna stand in my way of sayin' them, so, baby, please let me in.*

She hummed it. Then sang it under her breath.

The sidewalk was crowded. Church services had just let out, and the congregation moved through town, headed to picnics and sharing lunch with friends at one of the diners along the main street of Reedy. The boot shop was always busy on a Sunday afternoon, and today was no different.

Nola found her sister kneeling in a heap of boot boxes, smiling up at Jamie Poe, who seemed to be frequenting the shop more and more. The cowboy who never smiled but only glared his way into the wet dreams of most young girls in Reedy. And Molly obviously couldn't be happier.

"Not sure these ones are right," he was saying, blond hair hanging deliciously over smoldering green eyes.

"Well, you've tried on everything in your size in the past three days. I'm fresh out of stock. You're sure those Ferrinis felt too tight? They looked divine." Molly spotted Nola lurking nearby and shot her a dark look.

Nola flounced off to the opposite end of the store to give Molly space to flirt. Nola sifted through a few racks of clothes. Interest sparked in her. It had been too long since she'd spent time on the old things in her life. She couldn't spend much if

160

she wanted to keep that fat savings account for Nashville, but maybe a pretty new top would boost her mood.

She paused at that, her hand on a denim halter. *What's wrong with me? I* am *in a bad mood.*

Because Griffin had sent her away. Since the night they'd danced in the rain, he'd been totally different. Less burdened somehow, with plenty of smiles and his laughter ringing through the house. Alice had more energy, and even Lyric seemed to blossom under the happy canopy he'd thrown over the house.

He still ordered Nola around, but only in the best of ways— to get together a picnic for the four of them. To let him fold the basket of baby clothes because she looked bushed.

And to lay down on the wildflower petals he'd scattered over his bed so he could make her come again and again.

She shivered and brushed her hair off her face. Being sent away didn't sit well with her.

Gathering a handful of tops, she headed for the dressing room, situated near the place where Molly was still waiting on Jamie Poe. Her sister's voice had dipped to that honeyed drawl. Boy, she was really pouring it on today.

Nola rolled her eyes and zipped herself into the denim halter. She fluffed her hair and twisted left and right. Her breasts were propped up perfectly on the fabric, displaying golden cleavage Griffin would have a hard time resisting.

Wait. What the hell was she thinking? The old Nola wouldn't give a damn what man liked her in this top but how it looked from all angles on stage. She gripped the zipper on her side and ripped it down. She wriggled out of the tight fabric and replaced it on the hanger.

She reached for another shirt, but stopped at a glimpse of herself in the mirror. Her skin was bronzed and smooth. Griffin hadn't given her another mark since she'd voiced her displeasure over it, but now she longed to see a beard burn or a

161

bright red kiss mark.

Disgusted with herself, she abandoned all thoughts of trying on more tops. She redressed and exited the fitting room just as Jamie Poe was walking out the door.

Molly's red brows were drawn in irritation. "I suppose you heard everything."

"No. Once I shut the dressing room door, I couldn't hear you anymore." *Or I only was thinking of my own love story.*

Molly's expression lightened and she gestured to the clothes in Nola's hand. "You like any of those?"

"Nah. I'm not in the mood to shop, I guess."

Her sister took the garments and hung them on a rack to put away later. Then she started collecting the boxes Jamie Poe had left behind. Nola watched her for a moment then drifted to the wall of boots. Thousands of dollars' worth of leather graced the wall, ranging from utilitarian rancher's boots to the finest Tony Lamas.

Nola looked over the women's selection. A bright blue pair caught her eye.

Somethin' blue.

She stopped breathing. Before she knew it, she'd drifted forward to pull the boot from the small shelf. "Molly, you have these in—"

"A seven, yeah. You're gonna love them, sis. When we got the shipment, first thing I did was try them on and strut around the store. Hold on. I'll get 'em."

Nola turned the boot from side to side, admiring the pearly white insets that would match a wedding gown oh so well. Her heart chimed a wedding march but her mind added Griffin's lyrics.

By the time Molly returned, Nola was flustered.

"Why are you blushing?"

Nola ducked her head and sat abruptly on the cushioned

bench to pull off her sandals. "I'm not. It's hot in here."

"Whatever you say." Molly removed the boots from the box and handed her sister two peds for trying on the boots. "You been singing? You haven't been home for me to hear."

"Yeah, of course. I took my guitar to Griffin's, and I sing when the baby's asleep."

"Bet your man loves your voice. You have so much talent. Any guy would jump at the chance to have you." Molly looked wistfully toward the door Jamie Poe had vanished through.

Nola softened and put a hand on her sister's arm. "You have so much to offer too, Molly."

Her sister shook herself. "Doesn't matter, I guess."

"If you stop looking for love, it will drop into your lap. Everyone says that."

"Yeah, well, Mom and Dad don't know what they're talking about." She stuck out her tongue, and Nola laughed.

Then she slipped the boots on. They fit as though they'd been made for her. Little country elves in chaps had cut them out and sewn them to fit her feet. Or the fairy godmother had magicked them. Whatever had happened, these boots were made for Nola.

"Oh my God, Nola! Those boots were meant for you!"

Just as Molly had once said a cowboy with a daughter named Lyric was written in the stars.

Nola's heart turned over. "I'll take them."

Molly's eyes flared wide. "You don't know how much they are!"

"I saw the price on the box. I'm splurging. Sometimes you can't pass up something so perfect when it falls into your lap."

Molly's mouth tipped into a sly smile. "I have a feeling we're not only talking about boots. But okay, I'll write them up. Thanks for the commission."

# Chapter Thirteen

Griffin watched the last of the farm implements he was selling rattle away in the back of a farmer's truck. He told himself he hadn't needed those old tractor attachments or mowing decks. But fact was, he hated selling his stuff.

No, that wasn't entirely true. He hadn't minded giving up the motorcycle to Taylor. That money had paid Miranda's tuition and housing for the year, a few bills he was behind on and got him four new horses. A small nest egg waited for him to buy a ring, but he'd been stalling.

Now he was selling items to put a nice buffer back into his bank account. He hated running on empty.

His ma was still in the hospital after a successful surgery, but he was run ragged between ranch, daughter and hospital. And to make things worse, Nola had been distant with him.

He felt her slipping away by the minute. She had enough money to leave.

"I need to do Nashville, Griffin. I know you understand."

He'd stared at her profile. She lay in his bed—he could still taste her arousal on his lips. He sure as hell didn't understand what was going on between them or how they would possibly end in anything but heartache.

He skimmed her torso with the flat of his hand. "When will you go?"

She pivoted her head to look at him. The expression in her eyes made his stomach plummet. "I know you're hoping your ma can handle herself soon. And Lyric needs a nanny..."

Agitation ripped through his gut. He patted her hip. "Don't

you worry about us. You do what you need to do."

*Can't believe I said that.* It was five thousand miles away from what he needed to tell Nola. But for some reason the words were locked up in him. He'd convinced Miranda to drop her dreams for nine months—he couldn't ask Nola to do anything of the sort. His demands of Miranda—to have the baby, to marry him—got him single father status.

Fresh annoyance bombed any good feelings he may have possessed at having cash in his pocket. He closed the doors of the outbuilding and strode toward the house. The weather had finally turned, and steam ribboned from the ground as the sun burned off the dew.

Lyric had been cranky this morning, having awakened several times during the night. The last time, Griffin had rocked her for an hour before she'd finally drifted off. When he'd left her with Nola this morning, she'd been gnawing on her fists with the purpose of cutting a tooth.

He steeled himself to greet an equally grouchy Nola. He also needed to call his ma at the hospital and check in. Tonight he and Lyric would head into Reedy for a visit, but he had some chores to do around home first.

The new horses were thriving, but they needed a bigger space to roam. He had the fencing supplies. Now he needed the time to put into the task.

First he needed a cold drink.

His shirt clung damply to his shoulder blades. Swallowing hard at the thought of an ice-cold tea trickling down his throat, he increased his pace.

By the time he reached the house, he'd almost found some calm headspace. But when he discovered Lyric red-faced with rage in the baby seat, his mood rocketed into the stratosphere.

"Where's Nola?" He bent and unbuckled Lyric. As he lifted her, she kicked against him, wailing in his ear. He patted her back and went through the house, looking for Nola.

He called her name a few times before she emerged from the bathroom, still drying her hands on a towel. He took one look at her sweet, innocent face and hated himself for ever getting involved with her.

She'd leave Reedy and become a big-time star. He'd be a distant memory, a guy she'd hardly recall after some hot country celebrity got his hands on her.

"Why the hell did you leave Lyric all alone in the kitchen?"

Her face scorched. "I was going to the bathroom," she said through clenched teeth.

Ignoring her response, he whirled around and stomped through the house.

"You're leaving mud on the floors. I just vacuumed."

"Yeah, well, I was greeted by my daughter's screams. I didn't think to take off my boots."

"Well you should. She was fine. People have to walk away sometimes."

He knew she was right, but the snowball of agitation had already started rolling downhill. He slashed a hand through the air. "What about dishes? Did you make up bottles?"

Nola's mouth tightened. "I'm getting to it. Just because some people begin their day at the butt-crack of dawn doesn't mean all of us do."

He pushed a breath through his nose and rummaged around the freezer for a cold teething ring. Using it to plug Lyric's mouth, he glared at Nola. Last night she hadn't done more than give him a cold peck on the mouth, which was quite the departure from the wildcat who'd asked him to fuck her ass in the shower.

To make it worse, she'd shown up wearing a pair of new blue cowgirl boots that tormented the hell out of him. His cock jerked now just thinking about how her tanned calves had looked against that blue leather.

She glared back at him for a brief moment before spinning to the sink. With jerky movements she plugged the bowl and filled it with water so hot it made the hair at her temples curl.

"Oh, and your mother called. She'd like you to come down to the hospital before four o'clock because that's when the doctor makes his rounds."

"And you didn't think you should come out and tell me that?"

She glanced over her shoulder, giving him a clear look at her angry expression. "No. Why are you acting like such an ass?"

"Me? I'm trying to do my job, Nola. Take care of the ranch, a kid, my sick ma and you."

She whirled around and placed her wet, soapy hands on her hips. "Me?"

"Yeah." Goddammit, he wanted to take care of her in a thousand different ways. But she was drifting away from him on the sea that stretched between youth and weighed-down, middle-aged cowboy who couldn't bring himself to tether her to Reedy, to his ranch.

To him.

They stared at each other for a full minute. When he didn't respond to her, she shook her hands, flicking soap bubbles all over the floor. Then she strode into the mudroom.

He followed her, Lyric still in his arms and a black coal in his heart. "Where are you going?"

She shoved her feet into her blue cowgirl boots and twisted to look at him. "I'm leaving. I don't need to take this kind of abuse from an employer for taking a bathroom break. If I can't do your dishes right or take your messages to your satisfaction, I recommend finding someone who can."

With that she shot out the door. He strode after her, wanting so badly to catch her in his arms and apologize, to say he was the biggest idiot in the world. Or drop to his knees and beg her to marry him again.

But he stopped halfway to the driveway and watched her go.

The coal in his chest grew cold. He placed a kiss on Lyric's silky forehead and realized the sun was shining but he'd danced better in the rain.

"Have you called her?" His mother's voice was weak.

Griffin snapped his mind back and tore his gaze from the hospital window overlooking the parking lot. "No."

His ma pressed her lips together but said nothing.

Maybe he should call Nola. Or better yet show up at her house as he'd done before. Only this time he had no idea how to bridge the gulf he'd created between them.

He heaved a sigh. "You gonna be all right for the night, Ma? I have to make a stop for diapers on the way home." Lyric lay in his arms, fast asleep after a fussy day. Finally some pain reliever had zonked her out.

His ma gave a watery smile and nod. Her eyes drooped with fatigue, but she looked a hundred percent better than she had after her surgery a few days before. The doctor felt positive about her outlook, which was amazing news but somehow solidified the fact that Griffin was a total asshole.

The people in his life could disappear too easily.

"I'm gonna get going, Ma." He stood, and Lyric sighed in her sleep. He leaned in to kiss his mother on the cheek. "Love ya. I'll be back tomorrow. Get some rest."

"I will." That was all she said, but he heard *stop being a jerk* in his head.

When he got to the drugstore, Lyric had awakened. He got her out of the car seat and carried her into the store. She seemed content for the moment, but it was only a matter of time before her teeth started hurting again. He'd better pick up more pain meds.

He made a beeline for the diapers when he glimpsed red hair.

His heart lurched.

Not strawberry blonde. *Red, you dumbass.*

But when he approached, he saw it was Nola's sister. They looked right at each other, and a dark snake of knowing slithered through his stomach.

Molly moved toward him slowly. Her face was closed. Though she wasn't giving anything away, she didn't have to. He knew.

"She's gone, isn't she?"

Tears sprang to Molly's eyes, and she dropped her gaze. "Yes, today. She packed her car and took off right after lunch."

God, that long ago? How far could she have gotten in that amount of time? She'd be most of the way across Texas. Panic seized him.

Lyric squawked, and he lurched into action. "I'd best be on my way."

After making his purchases, he practically ran out of the store, away from the bearer of the news that made him ache. He got into the truck, barely breathing around the tears that clogged his throat or the hot knife of regret in his gut.

Nola was gone—on the road with the money he'd paid her, her guitar and a pipe dream.

He scrubbed both hands over his face. When he spoke to Lyric, his voice was strained. "Well, little girl, it's you and me again."

She blinked at him with wide eyes.

He folded his hand around her chubby fist inside his and shook it lightly. Moisture glazed his eyes as he thought of all he'd thrown away.


Nola sucked in a deep breath, filling her lungs to bursting. Then she flicked her fingers to release her nerves and let out all of her air. She pushed through the door of the music agent's office and was immediately dazzled.

Posters of country music legends plastered the walls along with framed gold records. The posh décor screamed money. And Nola was determined to be part of it.

She approached the long, shiny desk where the receptionist sat. The desk was lacquered a bright purple, so shiny Nola could catch her reflection in it. Even the employee looked like a celebrity.

Nola smoothed her hand over her skirt nervously. She'd gone all-out with her attire today. A gauzy skirt, fitted corset top and her new blue cowgirl boots for luck. The leather belt around her hips looked as if a country song might have been written for it, and the bracelets lining her wrist completed the ensemble.

She'd spent two hours culling this costume for five minutes in the agent's office. And she wouldn't even get to see him today. Her voice had won her this chance, and she had to emanate country music from head to toe. In the end though, the flash drive locked in her fist would get her through those double doors.

Channeling that confidence, she gave her best smile.

"Yes?"

"Nola Brady. I'm dropping off a flash drive as requested."

The woman's jacket had to have cost as much as Nola's car. Suddenly she wondered if she looked nice enough. Even the receptionist's lipstick looked expensive. Nola's had come from the Reedy drugstore clearance bin.

A deep ache for her hometown began in her core. She'd never been away from her happy family for this long. After a month, she found she missed other things she never dreamed of too—the sun sinking low over the mountains surrounding the sleepy town. The crush of summer tourists. She missed The Hellion on karaoke night even though she'd belted out a song in a different hotspot every night here in Nashville.

The Nashville crowds seemed to respond as well as the Reedy ones. Sooner or later she was banking on an agent or talent scout being in the audience.

When the receptionist checked her computer screen, Nola swallowed her nervousness. "Yes, you're on the list. I'll take the flash drive."

Nola held out the silver device and dropped it onto the woman's smooth palm. Her manicured nails closed around it.

"You'll hear from us within a week if we're interested. Good luck." Something about the way the employee said that made Nola think of home. Maybe because her tone was genuine, and Nola hadn't encountered that very often in the past month.

She thanked the receptionist and headed back out of the office, crossing her fingers and toes that this was it. Hell, she'd even cross her eyes all the way down in the elevator if it helped.

The thought made her think of Molly, who'd been a master eye crosser as a kid. Their mother had battled an entire year of first grade where Molly looked at everyone like a half-wit, tongue lolling to the side and eyes crossed. Even her school picture had sported slightly crossed eyes.

Nola made the ride down to the ground level. Then she strode through the sleek lobby to the glass doors. Each day some of her fears trickled away as she learned a new street, a new pub or little opry tucked in an obscure section of town.

That first day she'd arrived, she'd almost peed her pants with excitement and terror. *And heartbreak. Can't forget that.*

If Griffin had asked her to marry him again, she would

have said yes. In fact she'd waited for it day and night, but in the end he'd only pushed her away.

She firmly shoved that burning ache in her chest down and slammed a door on it. Locking it into a vault was the only way she could deal with it. On the cross-country drive she'd shed enough tears for a lifetime. The old trail of tears.

Pushing through the doors outside, she drank in the bustle of the city and tried to rid herself of her desire for a place called Needle's Pass.

She was better off here, pursuing her dream. In the time she'd been here, she'd entered four contests and gotten recognition. In a bar called Belts and Boots, she'd placed in their monthly contest, which had earned her the right to pass along a sample of her music to an agent.

A thrill hit her belly at what she'd just done.

This could be it. Her break.

She wandered down the sidewalk, staring at her surroundings. Between the architecture and the culture change, she was enraptured with Nashville. After only two weeks she'd run out of money and had to snag a waitressing job, but she didn't even mind that. Talking to people was fun, you never knew who you'd end up serving...and it reminded her of home.

Releasing a sigh, she admitted to herself it was probably time to call her family. She tried to keep those calls to a minimum. Never emotional, her father was short on the phone, asking about her job and the economy apartment she rented. She let him believe it was a decent place to live, but really she hated the peeling wallpaper and the noise from the other tenants.

No, she hated it because she'd heard gunshots on more than one night, and just being in the place made her bowels turn to water. When she didn't need to sleep, she avoided it at all costs.

172

On the phone her mother sounded weepy and asked about her diet. Was she eating well? Did she have enough?

Nola had assured her that yes, she was getting a discount at the restaurant, and there was plenty of fresh fruit and vegetables in Tennessee.

But talking to Molly...that really gutted Nola. Because the day she'd left, Nola had blubbered all over the place and confided her love for Griffin.

Molly shook her head in dazed awe. "Well, that's awesome, Nola!"

"No, it's not," she'd spat, throwing a fistful of bras into her suitcase. "Love isn't beautiful or a fairy tale. It's a pain in the ass."

"Why? Because you can't take it to Nashville with you?" Molly picked up a bra and dangled it from her finger. "I'm sure you can pack it away inside your heart. Come back for weekend flings with Griffin and have video sex when you're apart."

Nola battled her tears. Her nose was clogged and her skin too hot, too tight. She wanted to unzip it, peel it off and discard it like a chrysalis. Then she could really fly in Nashville.

"It's not going to work with Griffin. He doesn't like me."

"What?" Molly sat on the bed.

"He just..." Nola gave up trying to neatly fold a pair of jeans and wadded them in the bottom of the suitcase. She glanced at Molly's compassionate expression and almost broke down. "He thinks I'm young and incompetent. I don't do the dishes when I should or do right by Lyric."

"He hasn't complained all this time you've been working for him."

"Oh yes, he has. And today was the last time."

Nola jerked herself from the memory. Tears stung, and she wished she could suck them back in. As carefully as possible she ran her forefingers under her eyes, trying not to disturb her

173

mascara. This afternoon she planned to camp out in another music executive's office and get some attention.

She crossed the street and headed down a tree-lined stretch. As she passed a silver birch tree, she dragged her fingers across the bark and tipped her face up to stare at the leaves.

God, she wanted Griffin. Right now, what would he be doing? Was he happy? Were Lyric and Alice thriving?

Molly would know.

That's exactly why Nola didn't want to call her.

Yet every cell in her being longed to.

*I'm a mess.*

She drifted toward a park bench. As she reached it, two young guys eyed her. Good old boys wearing jeans and T-shirts, reminding her too much of home.

"Love the boots," one commented with a flick of his head.

"Thanks." She had a love-hate relationship with these boots. They represented all the hopes she'd hung on Griffin. A path she'd never dreamed she'd follow. Yet he'd gripped her tight and pulled her down the path only to show her it was a dead end.

"You gotta be a singer. You just look like a singer."

She smiled at the feeling of warmth his words infused. "I am."

"Let me guess. You're fresh off the bus, looking for a big break," the other guy said. He was dark-haired and brown-eyed. Griffin's coloring, but compared to the man she loved, these guys looked like high school kids.

Damn, she really was tainted forever.

"I'm pursuing my singing career, yes."

"We know of a few places talent scouts frequent. We could probably get you in."

"Yeah?" Her rule of always being polite had paid off more

than once in this town.

"You got a phone?" The first guy pulled his from his back pocket.

Nola blinked at it, expecting to see a baby monitor. Her throat closed off. Dipping her head, she rummaged in her purse for her cell. "Right here."

"Add my number. Call me tonight and I'll give you a list of places you can try."

"Thanks." She smiled, but it felt wrong on her face—wobbly, splatted on with glue that didn't do the job. The smile slid off her face, and she didn't try to put it back. She added the guy's number and gave a parting wave.

Then she continued on down the street. Her thumb roved over the keys of her cell on its own. She brought it to her ear. "Molly."

"Can't talk now, sis. I'm with a customer."

Nola's heart plummeted. She dragged her feet, scraping her heels on the sidewalk. What she wouldn't give to be knee-deep in the field with her hand in Griffin's and Lyric in her arm right now.

She started crying.

Molly's voice projected into her ear, frenzied and guilt-ridden at once. "Oh hey, I'm sorry. I can talk. Mitchell, you're doin' all right there on your own, aren't ya? Yeah, I thought. Okay, Nola. What's going on?"

Nola gave a huge sniff.

"You're failing."

"What? No, I just got started. I'd hardly call it a failure yet."

"You thought you'd jump right onto the scene with a big record deal."

"No, I never thought that—"

Her sister cut her off. "Now you've realized what you had here wasn't so bad. That there are other dreams worth

175

pursuing."

"Oh shut up, Molly." Her tears vanished, replaced by anger. "You don't know anything about it. I'm sorry I called you."

"I know you only called to probe for information about Griffin."

Nola stopped breathing.

"So I'm not wrong."

Nola heard Molly shuffling hangers as she probably revolved through the store, straightening merchandise. She wanted to ask about Griffin, but her stubborn will kept her from opening her mouth.

Finally Molly said, "Have it your way. Don't ask. I've gotta run now, Nola. Mitchell's ready to check out."

The phone clicked, and Nola growled. She stared at the digital display for a minute, unsure whether to hurl the phone into the gutter or get her sister back on the line. Dammit, Nola did want to hear about Griffin.

She dropped her phone into her purse again and hurried on. If she arrived at the music executive's office around lunchtime, she might get a glimpse of him. All she needed was one person to talk to her, listen to her sing, give her a chance. She was sure of it.

She also possessed a bone-deep surety that Griffin was not okay either. What had he told her once? *I don't do long nights well.*

Since leaving, Nola had asked herself dozens of times whether he loved her or just having someone near. She was convenient. A single dad didn't get a lot of dating opportunities. She'd fallen into his arms at The Hellion that night, then later into his lap when he took her home.

Nola had taken on the role of mother to Lyric, which obviously appealed to Griffin. And too easily she'd slipped into his bed and become his lover.

Any woman might have fulfilled his needs.

She fought her emotions and headed into a corner store for a bottle of sweet tea. But even slaking her thirst reminded her of Griffin because he made better sweet tea.

"Dammit." She screwed the cap on with a jerk of her wrist. Disgusted with herself, she steeled her resolve and set out for the executive's office. She would forget about her failed relationship and dashed dreams of tying herself to that man. And she'd return to her first love—singing.

An hour later she posed against a column in the lobby of the exec's office, hoping he'd come out and ask her name. Her purse was filled with flash drives. She'd hand him one and he'd nod and smile. Then he'd ask her to join him for lunch, where she'd convince him she was the hottest new talent country music had seen in a decade.

But late in the afternoon, she gave up and let her fantasy swirl down the mental toilet. No one was going to see her, and she had to be at work in an hour.

Rushing across town to her apartment only made her feel more strung-out. By the time she donned her uniform of swingy denim skirt, plaid top and felt cowgirl hat, she was ready for a soak in a hot bath.

*Damn, even that makes me think of Griffin.*

With a growl, she locked her apartment and turned to run down the flight of stairs. Her ring tone blared from the depths of her purse, and she dug around for it without looking.

"Yeah?"

"Umm...Miss Brady?"

Her heart spasmed at the unfamiliar voice. "Yes, it's Nola."

"Mr. Duvall has listened to your flash drive and would like to invite you to audition for him. Tuesday at 7:00 p.m."

Nola fist-punched the air and contained her shriek of glee. "That's so exciting." *Don't scream. Don't scream.* "I'll be there.

Thank you."

After ending the call, she stared at the caller ID for ten full seconds. Yes, it was real. She had an audition.

At work she spread her grins and good mood all over the place and earned two hundred dollars in tips. It was the best day of her life.

Except she didn't have anyone to share it with.

Tuesday at exactly 7:01 p.m., Nola sank to a leather sofa in the agent's private office with her guitar and wearing her best country star outfit. She'd spent days rehearsing her song. Now she'd wow them with not only her voice but her writing abilities.

But when she opened her mouth, the first line of Griffin's song burst from her.

# Chapter Fourteen

The Reedy grocery store boasted exactly two square feet worth of baby food. The glass jars were lined up on two shelves, perfect rows with labels facing forward.

Griffin stared at them, at a loss for what to do. The books all said to start babies on bland vegetables first. But his first attempt at giving Lyric carrots had ended with him sporting orange polka dots. Same with green beans.

"Whattaya think, little girl? Does squash sound good?"

Lyric sat up in the shopping cart, chubby fists wrapped around the handle. She kicked her little socked feet and gave him a two-toothed grin. At six months old, she'd suddenly learned how to sit up and popped two new teeth in a week. Now at eight months she was terrorizing Griffin by dragging herself across the floor.

"Today it's baby food. Tomorrow skinny jeans. Gah." He rubbed a hand over his face and resumed his perusal of the jarred food. His ma had recommended ignoring the pediatrician's advice to go slowly and try one food at a time, and just give Lyric several new foods at once.

Griffin liked the smorgasbord idea, but what if Lyric had a food reaction? Then he wouldn't know what she was allergic to.

"You don't like anything anyhow," he muttered. Plucking a jar off the shelf, he turned it to read the label. It had roasted sweet potato flavor. Was it flavor or real sweet potatoes? Hell, he could cook a potato. Maybe he needed to forget about jars and get down to basics.

Lyric squealed, and a lady pushing a cart past them

stopped to smile. "Aren't you the sweetest little thing? I'm sure Daddy has his hands full with you."

Griffin centered his gaze on the woman. She was in her late thirties, her warm brown hair grazing her shoulders in soft waves. He didn't know her, but he'd seen her around town.

She turned her smile onto Griffin. "Sorry, I've heard about you and your daughter." She caught Lyric's hand. When the baby directed the woman's finger toward her mouth, the lady pulled it free with a laugh.

Griffin looked at her more closely. "What have you heard?" *How I've been a basket case since Nola left town?*

He'd basically become a recluse, and for him, that was saying something. When he drove his ma to the doctor, he didn't speak to anyone. No more standing on the corner by the drugstore, talking cattle prices with the guys. And he hadn't spoken to Taylor in too long.

Griffin's ma had tried to discuss the subject of Nola, but he'd shut her right down. He didn't need to hear about how he should get out there again and find someone new to date.

"I'm sorry. I didn't introduce myself. I'm Katherine." The shopper extended her hand, and Griffin shook it.

"Griffin."

"I know."

That wasn't good. Was he becoming the guy people in town gossiped about? Old Turner, sitting up there with his sick ma and a baby, pining over that Brady girl. Christ, he might be.

Hell, that's exactly what he was.

Katherine had the grace to blush. "My sister is a nurse in the chemo clinic. She's spoken of you coming in with your mother and daughter."

"Ah, I see." So Katherine hadn't heard the gossip in church or the lady's guild meeting. He breathed a sigh of relief.

She gestured to the baby food. "She's just starting foods,

right?"

"Yes, and she hates them all. Last week we tried a few, but she won't keep any in her mouth." And no wonder—it tasted awful. Would it be so difficult to mix in some butter and salt?

Katherine gave a short laugh and bent to talk to Lyric. "Are you being naughty and giving your daddy a hard time?"

Griffin's stomach dropped out as if he'd just taken a wild turn on a bull. Memories of Nola bent over Lyric, cooing and talking to the baby as if she understood every word, rolled through his head.

He fought down a rising lump in his throat. Suddenly he wanted nothing more than to escape the grocery store and this woman. She was nice enough, yes, and pretty in her own right. And she was obviously interested in him, which set off alarm bells in his head.

He wanted to back away, hands up, and warn her off him. He didn't do well with relationships and had managed to drive away the best woman who'd ever entered his life.

"I think we'll just try these." Griffin grabbed about ten miscellaneous jars and placed them in the cart. "Thanks for chatting, but we have to get back home."

Katherine eyed him as if she was about to say something, but he hightailed it to the front of the store, far away from female attention. Every bone in his body craved a certain little country singer, and he couldn't stick around and risk Katherine asking him out.

When he got home, his ma took one look at him and recognized his panic. She came forward to take Lyric from him, and he set the grocery bag on the table with a small clunk.

"Don't you think it's time to give up the stubborn cowboy ruse and just call her?"

"What?" He jammed a hand through his hair, pretending she shocked him with her question.

She settled Lyric on her hip and released the Velcro strap on the baby's bonnet. "You're surly, Griffin Edward Turner."

He shot her a look. "Oh, I get all three names?"

"When you're not listening to your inner voices, that's the only way to get your attention. Remember when you were sixteen and determined to jump that cliff on your dirt bike?"

"Odds were twenty to one on me." Half the school had been rallied around him, cheering him on. Only one other person in Reedy had completed the jump. Personally Griffin wasn't afraid of the gap. Falling to his death in the rocky ravine was never a question in his mind, because the jump was more about having the guts to try it.

His mother went on. "I had to get your attention then, and I'll damn well get it now."

He looked at her hard. Her appearance was improving daily, and she was no longer acting like a shell-shocked victim of a dreaded disease. He secretly believed half of her battle had been mental—just like the cliff jump. Once she figured out she could survive her cancer, she made up her mind to go on living.

Suddenly yearning broke over him. For Nola. For his youth.

For that dirt bike.

How reckless he'd been as a teen. Even in his twenties, no one rivaled his lust for life. He threw himself into every venture without even checking the depth of the water. But somewhere along the lines he'd lost that fervor.

He'd like to call himself a cautious single father, but that wasn't it. He hadn't truly embraced life in far too long. Although he'd given Nola a few impulsive moments.

"Ma, can you keep Lyric?"

She blinked at him and shifted the baby to the other hip. "I guess so." She narrowed her eyes. "What are you planning?"

He let his gaze linger on Lyric. In the eight months since her birth, he'd given up plenty, and gained more. He wasn't willing to put her in a glass bubble either.

"Give her the baby food smorgasbord tonight, Ma. I'll be back in a few hours."

"Oookay."

He walked into the mudroom and found a pair of leather gloves. *In case I have to climb out of a ravine.* His mother followed him, distress creasing her eyes. He leaned in and pecked her on the cheek. "Don't worry. I'll be back. Tell me which food Lyric likes better."

Outside, he strode straight to the barn. He might not own a dirt bike anymore, but he had something just as good. Bart.

The horse wasn't lazing, eyes half-closed in snoozing bliss. No, the stallion was waiting for Griffin as if he'd predicted this moment.

"Ready, boy?" Griffin grabbed a bridle and fitted it on the horse. Then he led Bart from the stall into the sun. Gripping the horse's mane, he swung bareback onto the animal. "Hope you're feeling energetic today. Yaw!"

He galloped across the fields, angling upward so the horse didn't tire running straight uphill. Bart's muscles coiled and released under him, and Griffin let his mind go. They carved a path through the high grasses. When the terrain turned rockier, he slowed Bart a little.

As the intermittent stones gave way to rock, Griffin gazed out over the landscape. This was one of the highest points in Needle's Pass. He and Taylor had spent many an evening here with their girlfriends and a six-pack. Judging from the remains of a campfire, the peak still lured people.

He dismounted and walked a hundred yards to the ledge. The jagged rocks jutted from the earth, extending in a sort of false shelf and giving the illusion one could walk out on it and cross the gap to the other side. In total the jump was only about seven feet. If you stood on the ledge, you'd be closer. But the shelf wouldn't hold his weight.

Besides, he was determined to jump it. His ma had put a stop to his glory all those years ago, but not now.

He walked back to Bart. Running a hand down the animal's soft coat, he gathered his courage. A misstep would land him fifty feet down. If he went and got himself killed, what would happen to Lyric?

He could only think of one person he'd want to raise her, and that galvanized him into action.

*I'm going to jump this goddamn ravine. Then I'll go home and call Nola.*

When he spurred Bart on, he allowed the horse its head. The best way to make the jump was mindlessly. He had to be one with the animal and not give a thought to stride length or timing.

They'd make it or wouldn't.

Just as he and Nola would. But he was done fucking around.

Bart ground the rock under his hooves as he made the run. The horse dug in. Sprang. Griffin felt a smile spread over his face as the horse leaped.

All those years ago he'd thought about looking down as he jumped. But now that he was mid-flight, he didn't give a damn what was at the bottom. He looked at the sky.

Nola poured every ounce of homesickness and love she felt for Griffin into that song. That damn song she wasn't supposed to sing.

The one that got the record deal.

How was she going to tell Griffin she'd stolen his song and sold it to Nashville?

She flopped on her bed face down. The past two weeks had been a whirlwind of phone calls and texts with the agent. The record company had big plans for her, loved her look, her voice, what she stood for. Apparently her home-grown qualities appealed to the masses right now, and the company wanted to strike before the branding iron cooled.

For the thousandth time she contemplated her situation. This was why she'd come to Nashville, but now that she was neck-deep in recording sessions and contracts, terror seized her.

She'd sworn her family to secrecy about the news, in case something fell through. Sort of like having a miscarriage. If she never birthed this career, she didn't want to explain it to the world.

And how the hell was she going to make the most important person understand? Griffin would never speak to her again.

Her cell rang, and she glared at it. Last week she'd made a certain song the ring tone for the agent's office and had regretted it ever since.

Turned out the polished receptionist's name was Jessica, and she was now Nola's number one fan. And Jessica called dozens of times a day. Nola longed for peace and quiet. A rocking chair on a wide front porch and a cold beer in hand.

Griffin's kisses.

Stifling a groan, she grabbed the cell.

"Hi, Nola, it's Jessica."

*I know.*

"There's a party tonight at the house of one of the execs. Bryant would like you to be there."

Nola glanced at the wall calendar where her work shift was indicated in red marker. "I have to work."

"No, no, no, no. You're big time now, girl! Bryant says to get your bikini on and he'll pick you up at seven-thirty."

"I don't have a bikini." Hell, she didn't even have a

185

swimsuit. When packing for Nashville, she hadn't given a thought to swimwear.

"Then we'll have to go shopping! Come at lunchtime. We'll hit the shops."

Jessica was tireless in her quest to give Nola the best chances. But everything felt wrong. Namely a single about to be released with her name on it, which she did not write.

"Okay, I'll meet you for shopping. But I need to talk to you about that song. 'One Lyric' shouldn't be released first. I'm thinking 'Girl with a Gun' should be the first single." Nola gripped the phone, prepared for Jessica's laughter.

Bryant had laughed at her too. "C'mon, Nola. The song is perfect. A ballad like that is a sure hit, and you need to leap into the waters with it. Let those sharks know who has the prettiest teeth. I know Bryant spoke with you about this issue. We don't understand why you're stalling—"

*Because it's not my song.*

Jessica went on. "The song is perfect for a debut. Wait until you hear it after the recording studio mixes it. We're always right about these things."

*If Griffin wasn't totally lost to me before, he is now.* He would never come after her with a copyright lawsuit, only despise her privately.

Nola swiped her knuckles over her eyes. "All right. Whatever you say. I'll see you in a few hours."

She ended the call and buried her face in the covers. Dragging in a deep breath, she wished for a nose full of Griffin's spicy scent. Leather and hardworking man. Her body reacted with instant arousal.

On the night she'd signed the deal to release his song, he'd called her. Guilt and self-disgust had kept her from answering her phone. If she could kick her own ass with those adorable blue boots, she would. He deserved to know.

And she needed to know why he was calling. Instead of speaking with him, she'd phoned Molly and probed for information, but her sister knew nothing of Lyric, Alice or the man who held Nola's heart.

Biting down on her lip, she stared at the ceiling. She could call him now. But what to say?

*Hey, Griffin. Sorry I ran off. I'd hoped you would ask me to marry you for what—the third or fourth time? Then I missed you so much that your song just came out of me. And guess what? Now I'm going to make thousands of dollars on those lyrics you taught me while your cock was buried deep inside me. Oh yeah, and I'm not giving you credit for it.*

She yanked herself off the bed and headed to the shower. Chances were she didn't have enough cash in her account for any bikini Jessica would choose. Her taste was Angus steak on Nola's hamburger budget. That meant charging a bikini to her emergency credit card. Until her first advance came through for the record deal, she still pinched pennies.

Plus she had to call off work tonight—again—which would probably get her fired.

She prayed some money came through fast. On the other hand, she dreaded the release of that song.

Hours later she and Jessica were browsing the racks of a posh store. "This one?" Jessica held up a white string bikini.

"No." Nola scrunched her nose.

"That's the fifth one you've turned down. You'd look amazing in it. What's the problem?"

"It's just not what I'm looking for." What she meant was nothing looked like the garments sold in the store where Molly worked. Nola pictured something sleek with a hint of country rock. Silver conchos or even some rhinestones. These bikinis looked like city girls trying to be country.

*What am I thinking? Country girls skinny dip.*

Em Petrova

Heat washed over her flesh at the thought of a chance to skinny dip with Griffin.

Jessica thrust half a dozen suits into Nola's hands. "Go to the dressing room."

No point in arguing. Nola slipped behind the curtain and peeled off her clothes. As she tried on each bikini, she could only imagine Griffin's reaction to them.

Baby blue with a thong bottom?

*No fucking way. That's my ass.*

Red strappy top and high-cut briefs?

*I love you in red, baby doll.*

Her nipples hardened. As swiftly as possible she slipped on another. Her hair straggled over her shoulder in a loose ponytail, and she swept it back to get a better look at the leopard print bandeau top and matching bottoms.

It said new country with a serious dose of wildcat.

Griffin's eyes would be hooded with desire. And that's exactly what she wanted.

Jessica was thrilled with her decision, and they headed for the checkout. But on the way, they passed a table with itty bitty garments, items Nola was so familiar with folding. Onesies and little jeans. Footed pajamas with a cartoon rodeo bull on the front.

"Nola?" Jessica said over her shoulder.

"Just a minute." She picked up a pair of felt booties made to look like infant-sized cowgirl boots. Cobalt blue with silver thread detailing.

Nola's heart contracted, and tears jumped to her eyes. At one time she'd fantasized about Lyric toddling down the aisle ahead of her, headed straight for her daddy's arms. Then Griffin would scoop up his daughter and lock gazes with Nola.

The world would stop rotating in that moment when they accepted their futures were finally about to be meshed together.

188

A fat tear splashed down Nola's cheek.

"I need to head back to the office. Bryant has someone coming in this afternoon," Jessica complained.

Nola cradled the boots, not bothering to dash away the tear. As she paid for the overpriced bikini and the boots, Jessica shot her confused glances.

"For a special little someone," she said quietly, avoiding Jessica's gaze. Someone so special she couldn't bring herself to share her with Nashville. No, Lyric belonged back in Wyoming with her daddy.

*And their song has no business here either.*

# Chapter Fifteen

"Come on, Lyric. Come here." Griffin encouraged his daughter by waving his hands.

Lyric got up on all fours and rocked back and forth. He laughed at what he called her "revving her engine pose". She crawled like crazy to the coffee table and pulled herself up. For a week she'd been about to let go and take a step, and he couldn't wait. The faster she walked, the sooner he wouldn't be so tied to the house. His little girl could tag behind him and he could explain the world to her.

So many exciting things to teach her, such as how to keep her fingers flat when feeding a horse a carrot. Or where the whippoorwills hid their nests.

He wished he could explain why Nola hadn't taken his call that night months ago or bothered to call him back, as he'd requested in the voice message.

He passed his hand over his face, wishing he could wipe the pain from his heart. While he sat in Needle's Pass pining over her, she was probably having the time of her life in Nashville.

Hell, he hoped that was the case. He just wished she hadn't forgotten about him so thoroughly.

Lyric dug her toes into the carpet and launched forward. For a precarious moment he thought she might do a face dive. But she gave an excited whoop of laughter and shot toward him.

He held out his hands. "Come on! You're doin' it! What a good girl."

Her hair was getting thicker, and he'd been experimenting with a tiny ponytail on top of her head. It stuck straight up, and everyone who saw it smiled a little bigger. The new nanny had oohed and aahed over it.

The woman was in her sixties, a grandma whose grandbabies lived halfway across the world, part of a military family. Tessa had taken over Lyric's care without a bat of an eye. No instruction from Griffin was necessary.

Recalling those first days with Nola made his heart pang. He looked into his daughter's happy eyes and tried to imagine what it would be like for Lyric to grow up with a woman in her life. It was only a matter of time before his fumbling efforts at a ponytail no longer did the trick.

The baby was two short-legged steps from his open arms, but she came to a dead stop in order to pick a piece of lint off the carpet. She plopped onto her behind, pinched the fuzz between thumb and forefinger and directed it right at her mouth.

"Nooo." He tried to get it, but she was too quick and popped it into her mouth. "You know what this means, don't ya? You're getting the finger sweep you hate." He dug through her mouth for the lint, and she squirmed and grew red-faced. "If you don't like it, quit eating stuff off the floor." Between him and Tessa, they were vacuuming daily, but it wasn't enough. No lint was safe when Lyric was in the room.

"Oh there's my precious girl," his ma said from the doorway between kitchen and living room.

He looked up and gave her a crooked grin. She was improving. Not healed, but so much better. Living on her own again, doing for herself. Just being on her feet again made her stronger, it seemed.

Hooking an arm around Lyric's middle, he swept her off the floor and gained his feet in one fluid motion. Lyric saw her nana and flapped like a baby bird about to fly the nest.

They shared a laugh, and for a moment, it was enough. Not having a mother figure was all right. Lyric would be okay.

"Come to Nana."

Griffin held Lyric like an airplane and swooped her close to his ma's hands. When his mother tried to catch her, he pulled back and Lyric giggled. It was a game they played, and one Lyric couldn't get enough of.

"Get over here, you flying baby," his ma scolded, eyes sparkling.

Griffin passed her close. His ma's fingers trailed over the baby just before he snatched her away. In the kitchen, the radio he'd forgotten was turned on switched songs.

And his heart stopped.

He almost dropped Lyric, and she squealed.

"Son?" His ma's concerned tone made him get a grip.

He tucked Lyric close to his body and ran into the kitchen. He reached for the radio and cranked up the volume. Nola's throaty tones reverberated through his kitchen, and she was singing his song.

His ma plastered a hand to her mouth. "Oh my God."

"It's her. And my song." He could have repeated it ten times and still not get the meaning. Just hearing her goddamned voice made him want to jump that cliff again.

Or storm Nashville with a ring in hand.

And a paddling in mind. *Damn her for taking that song!*

As Nola's voice dipped and grew fainter, invoking more emotion into the ending of the song than he'd ever dreamed possible, he couldn't deny it was perfect coming from her lips.

Except it was his song, crooned to her during lovemaking. And for Lyric. He could sing it for his ma too. Hell, the song was for every woman in his life he loved.

He didn't know much about the music industry, but for her to have that song recorded and already hitting the airwaves, she

192

must have been discovered pretty damn quickly.

Maybe that's why she didn't call back. She was knee-deep in her music. His heart jerked with hope.

He turned his gaze to his ma. She returned his stare, obviously as shocked as he was.

"You have to go, Griffin. The fact that you love that girl is written all over you. I've never seen you..." She swallowed hard and smiled. "Just go."

"I'll take Lyric."

"Yes. It's only right."

A grin spread over his face, and joy poured into his veins, shooting him into motion. "Help me pack."

"Of course. But give me that little airplane." His mother echoed his excitement.

He planted a noisy kiss on Lyric's head before gliding her outward. The baby's squealed in delight as his ma snagged her out of the air.


The instant the bell on the door of the boot shop announced Griffin's arrival, Molly was bearing down on him. As soon as she saw it was him though, panic crossed her face.

Yeah, Nola's success wasn't a surprise to her sister.

Griffin pulled the ring box from his pocket and snapped it open as Molly came to stop before him. Her gaze flickered from him to the ring, and she sucked in a breath.

"I need her address."

"You heard the song."

He nodded. "I don't know whether to put her over my knee for stealing that song—"

"Stealing?" Molly's voice raised in pitch.

"Yeah. That song's mine. I wrote it."

"Oh." Molly deflated before his eyes.

"Give me her address."

She glanced at the ring again. It was a platinum band with a fat white diamond solitaire flanked by two pink diamonds. He'd taken one look at it and envisioned it on his girl's hand.

When Molly hesitated another heartbeat, he snapped the ring box shut. "Fine. I'll find her on my own. Can't be that hard now that she's famous." He swung away.

"Hold on," Molly called to his back. "Let me write it down."

He trailed her to the counter, where she pulled out a slip of paper and jotted down the address from her phone display.

Meeting her gaze, he accepted the paper from her. "Thank you." His words were infused with genuine gratitude. He pocketed the paper and the ring.

"Wait. You're gonna take the baby with you, right?"

"I'm planning on it, why?"

She pushed a thick lock of red hair behind her ear in the same gesture Nola used, and his heart flexed. "I just think it's best. She's in love with your little girl as much as she's in love with you, Griffin. Once she's faced with both of you, she won't be able to turn you down."

He grinned so wide his cheeks ached. And he kept on grinning all the way to his truck parked in the street, then up the long, snaking road to Needle's Pass. There he gathered two bags of luggage and his infant daughter, gave his ma a kiss goodbye and headed to the airport.

To Nola.


Flicking her hands to rid herself of nerves, Nola cast a look over the park. This outdoor concert wasn't her first, but lordy, there were a lot of people. Only a few snatches of lawn were visible between the bodies, and a few people even sat in the branches of trees.

*All here for me.* That song had hurled her right onto the charts. She was currently sitting at number five, but it changed hourly. Jessica took it upon herself to text Nola with updates.

As she scanned the crowd and the band that was now officially hers, it was impossible not to realize the magnitude of her accomplishment.

*It was Griffin's song that put me here though.* Had he heard it on the radio yet? He often kept the radio on in the kitchen. His love of music was just one more thing she adored about him.

Four months away, and her heart still beat for him. In the days since being discovered, she'd met the hottest men in Nashville. Country music artists, music executives, videographers. She had a bodyguard with muscles any girl would drool over.

But Nola longed for a cowboy daddy.

She flicked her fingers again.

"You're on in five," the stage manager told her. She nodded.

Weather permitting, these concerts in the park were one of the highlights in Nashville. Yesterday she'd come down to watch—then meet—an artist she'd only once dreamed of seeing. Now she was about to stand in the same spot as that Country Music Award-winner.

Her heart throbbed faster. She wasn't opening with "One Lyric". No, she had four other songs to ramp up the crowd with, then she'd lay the ballad out for a grand ending.

"Two minutes, Nola."

She dragged a deep breath into her lungs and bounced on her blue boots. In the past few weeks, she'd grown more and more accustomed to being primped and dolled up for the public. Bryant had hired a stylist to dress her. She'd eaten at restaurants where she had no idea which fork to use first but had learned in no time.

Still, she longed for a big old rack of ribs she could pick up and sink her teeth into. She wished she hadn't missed Reedy's annual summer days, including a parade and a picnic in the high school football field. How would it have felt to put her hand into Griffin's and let him lead her around from booth to booth, buy her cotton candy and then kiss it from her lips?

"Break a leg, Nola."

She surged forward to the cheers of the crowd. Up front Jessica and Bryant stood smiling. She gave them a nod and strode right to the microphone. As she looped the guitar strap over herself, a sudden case of the jitters struck her.

*Calm down. Nothing different about this than singing in The Hellion.*

What she wouldn't give for her family to be in the crowd. Molly, her mother and father. They planned to come down in two weeks for her first big concert. It still stunned her that people were paying to hear her sing.

"Howdy, Nashville!" she cried into the microphone, and the crowd rippled with stomps and cheers. She strummed the first chord, and her nerves only increased. She let her gaze flick across the crowd.

A movement caught her eye—a dark head moving through the crowd. A man pushing his way to the front.

He looked up, and she met his gaze fully. Suddenly she felt more in the spotlight than she had in the eyes of five hundred people.

Griffin.

His hot stare sliced right through her. It hit her pussy and burned her with instant arousal. She sucked in a harsh breath and strummed again to cover the crazy spinning in her head.

He reached the front of the crowd, Lyric in his arms and a big bag slung over his shoulder. Nola's heart tripped out of control, and she barely kept her feet glued to the stage. More than anything she wanted to jump down and forget about the concert, the people, her agent...she wanted to rush into Griffin's arms.

Behind her, the band struck up, urging her to begin.

She opened her mouth, and the world vanished. She locked her attention on one man and sang for him. When his eyes slipped shut, she knew it was all worth it. She'd walked out, found her place in the world, and he'd come after her.

Grinning, she belted out the upbeat song the record label planned as her second release. The crowd responded by clapping and cheering. She strutted across the stage, playing to those who had shown up to see her today, but only two people were important to her.

Lyric had grown considerably. She sported a ponytail on top of her head that made Nola grin wider. Griffin rocked to the beat, and she let her gaze slide over his muscled form.

Broad shoulders were wedged between other onlookers, clad in a white western shirt—the one he'd worn that first day she'd set eyes on him at The Hellion. The one with the embroidery. At that time, she'd realized this was a man who knew who he was. Until then she'd only been with boys.

Now she realized she'd never be happy with anyone but Griffin. The whole universe belonged to him, and so did she.

She ripped through three more songs. Lyric got fired up for one, bouncing in his arms. After four months away, would the baby recognize Nola? The idea of the child being strange with her made Nola's throat tighten.

She sang through it and let her mind whirl. Once she finished singing, what would Griffin do?

The band struck the first notes of "One Lyric", and Nola stopped breathing. She couldn't do this, could she? Sing Griffin's song she'd stolen right in front of him?

*No, I'll sing it right to him.*

His smile faded, and his gaze never wavered from her. The crowd roared then stilled to hear the first words of a song made more beautiful because Griffin was here.

Still, he might have come to force her to recognize him as the songwriter. Maybe she was fooling herself, thinking that dark look he wore was passion and not fury.

She stumbled over a word, and he caught her eye. When he gave her an easy nod, she recovered by shooting through an octave of notes. The crowd cheered.

Everything but Griffin and Lyric vanished. She threw her head back and sang with all her heart, hoping the things she'd done could be forgiven. Knowing she'd long ago forgiven him for succumbing to the stresses he bore.

As the final note tumbled from her, she met his gaze once more. He turned and pushed through the crowd. She fumbled off her guitar and ·spat out a few quick words of thanks. She hoped it was enough. It had to be enough.

Rushing offstage, she shoved past the stage manager and a few others. Bryant was there, arms open. But she ignored him and frantically looked for the one person she needed as much as air.

Then suddenly he was there, bigger than life. Her bodyguard stepped between them, and Griffin skirted the man, reaching for Nola.

She squeezed around the guard and hurled herself right into Griffin's arms. Lyric's solid little body was squashed between them.

"Damn you for singing that song. I loved every goddamn minute of it."

"Four minutes and twelve seconds, actually," she said breathlessly. Shivers gripped her as she tilted her head to stare into his eyes.

Nothing but love shone for her. She made a noise in her throat, and he smashed his mouth to hers.

The first taste was bliss. She gulped in his scent, and he thrust his tongue between her lips. She drowned in his taste and feel. Every scorching flip of his tongue ratcheted up her need. A tight string pulled between nipples and pussy, making her throb.

He snaked a hand around her neck and hauled her deeper with every pass of his tongue. She dug her fingers into his shoulders. Lyric fisted Nola's hair, but even the sting on her scalp was perfect.

Tears leaked from the corners of her eyes.

Griffin broke away, panting hard. "I need to get you outta here."

"Yes," she breathed.

# Chapter Sixteen

Griffin's stomach bottomed out as he followed Nola through a crush of people. She stopped, smiled and autographed papers waving at her. Hearing her sing, seeing her onstage, had been a door opening to reality.

This was her life now.

Did he have a place in it? The way she'd kissed him said he did, but her polished appearance and the way she was already so comfortable with fame whispered otherwise.

Still, she'd clung to him, shaking. That couldn't be faked.

"You didn't ride your horse here, did ya?" she asked, throwing a smile over her shoulder at him.

His balls tightened. All he wanted was Nola under him, legs hooked around his ears as he made her voice rise and fall in the song of ecstasy. She was poured into a tight little white leather dress. Her breasts spilled from the top, but her ass...

He scrubbed a hand over his face in a battle for control. Her curves made his cock throb.

They broke through the crowd. Nola stopped to speak with a tall man who placed a familiar hand on her arm. Griffin wanted to bust his fingers.

But Nola looked back at Griffin, and his heart soared once more. The lights in her eyes were only for him. She reached for his hand, and he clamped his fingers around hers. "This is Griffin and Lyric. I won't be answering my phone for a little while, Bryant."

"Don't forget I need you in the office tomorrow to discuss—"

She waved him off. "I know, I know. I'll be there."

Griffin's throat tightened at the idea that her obligations were enormous. She wouldn't belong to him forever.

Suddenly the ring in his pocket felt all wrong. He couldn't ask her to marry him here. The event had to take place on Reedy soil. There, she was just a country girl and he a cowboy. Getting her away from this place to propose was the right course.

He shifted Lyric, and Nola led the way to a waiting car. The driver of the sleek black vehicle came around to open the back door, and Nola slid across the seat. Griffin got in too. The fact that Lyric wasn't in a child safety seat bothered him, but they would be crawling through city traffic. Hopefully nothing bad would happen.

Nola was staring at him. Her red-gold hair was shinier, slightly longer. The bangs dipped into her eyes, and he used a forefinger to push it back.

She quivered and dropped her gaze. "I'm so sorry about...the song, Griffin. It was wrong of me, and..."

He placed a hand over her fingers twisting together in her lap. "It sounds just right coming from your lips, baby doll."

She sucked in an uneven breath, and tears spilled from her eyes. "I never thought I'd hear you say that again."

He placed his mouth against her ear. "Baby doll, I'm going to get you under me and love you until you stop thinking I'm upset about the song. I love you, Nola. I want you."

When he pulled away, her ripe lips beckoned to him. He leaned in and took his time kissing her, letting the emotion build.

Lyric, bored with the entire event, released a squawk. Nola drew back, laughing. "Oh come here, you darling girl. I missed you so much!" She plucked the baby from his hold and deposited her in her lap. He could only think about that white leather and what would happen if Lyric's diaper leaked.

He moved to take her back, but Nola shot him a hard look. Then she gripped Lyric under the arms and held her up in front of her face. Nola buried her nose against the baby's belly, and Lyric giggled.

"Look how big you are. Why did you go on growing without me?"

His heart clenched at the remorse in Nola's voice. He wrapped an arm around her shoulders and drew her against his chest. "She's not the only one who went on growing. Your voice today, baby doll... God, you sounded amazing. And you look..." He waved his hand over her form-fitting dress and the blue boots that had been his torment back in his kitchen.

She lowered Lyric and pressed kisses over the baby's chubby cheeks. Then she directed her attention to Griffin.

"This is just paint on an old barn, Griffin."

He grinned at her words and trailed a finger over her collarbone. "I'm the old barn."

She caught his hand and threaded their fingers together. Tears glistened in her eyes. "If I could have wished for anything in the world, it's this."

The car stopped, and she looked past him, out of the tinted window. "This is my building. Let's go inside."

He raked his gaze over her creamy breasts bursting from her dress. "And hope Lyric's feeling very sleepy."

"I'm ready for bed myself," Nola whispered, her throaty tone igniting him.

He rushed her out of the vehicle. The driver now acted as bodyguard, riding in the elevator with them, then trailing them to the door of her condo. When Griffin gave him a certain look, the man finally left them.

Nola's door didn't have a key, but she entered a security code into a keypad. She got it wrong the first time and swore. Giving Griffin an embarrassed look, she said, "This is all new to me. We don't even lock our doors in Reedy."

He watched her punch in the numbers, realizing with a shock it was his phone number and birthday.

Pressure built in his chest. He wrapped his arms around her from behind just as she opened the door. The inside was sleek and new. She waved a hand. "It came furnished. Bryant found it."

Jealousy mounted inside him. "Bryant?"

"My agent. That man I was speaking with after the concert."

"Ah." In his arms, Lyric squirmed. He set her on the floor, and she took off across the carpet, hell-bent for a short black string on the plush white rug.

Nola dropped to her knees. "Oh my gosh, you're crawling! I've missed so much."

"Not too much. But she's been taking some steps too." He sank to the carpet beside her and hauled her into his arms. She melted against him. He cupped her ass and cradled her head as he slanted his mouth across hers.

She tasted of tears and mint—and him. He growled with possessiveness. He chased her tongue around her mouth, gathering all the flavors he'd craved these long, lonely months.

She rubbed against him, and his cock swelled against her hip. She dragged her mouth away. "I need you."

He shot a look at Lyric. She was on her hands and knees, fighting to pick up the black string. "Let me get some toys out of her bag. That should buy us enough time for a quickie." Maybe he shouldn't have brought her, but it was clear Nola loved seeing Lyric.

Nola scooted off him, and he unzipped the baby bag. He pulled out a blanket, which he stretched out on the floor. Then he scattered toys on it. Lyric grunted at him, still determined to pick up that string.

When he removed a bottle of formula from the cold pack

and set it on the blanket, she crawled as fast as she could for it.

Nola laughed, a full, rich sound. God, he'd missed that.

Lyric got the bottle and rolled onto her back to drink it, her feet up in the air.

"That should keep her occupied for a while." He yanked Nola into his arms and crawled on his knees for a long sofa about ten feet from Lyric. He lay Nola on the cushions and lowered himself atop her.

She moaned, wrapping her arms around him. He burned with the need to sink into her, to make her his. Rocking against her, he took her mouth. Their kiss was fire to dry kindling.

"Christ, I need you. Missed you. Love you." He swiped his tongue over hers and found the zipper on her spine. She arched upwards to give him access. Once he pulled it down to the crest of her buttocks, he slipped his hand into the opening. Her silky skin greeted his fingers.

She pulled off his shirt and bit into his shoulder. He groaned in appreciation, beyond even curse words now. His drive to take her was the only thought in his head.

In a flurry they undressed each other. He stripped off her boots and socks and licked her toes until she squirmed, then he unpeeled the white leather from her curvy form. "Fuck, you're not wearing anything but this leather."

"Nothing else fit in there with me." She grinned, and his heart turned over.

He kicked free of his boxers and jeans and poised his cock at her slick folds. "I want to lick you until you scream for me. But I can't wait."

"Don't wait." She pressed on his ass, directing the head of his cock between her pussy lips. His balls clenched with the need to blow.

"Baby doll." His whisper was ragged.

She met his gaze, and he sank an inch into her tight,

scorching hot sheath. Her eyes hazed with pleasure. "Yes?"

"Only one lyric is important enough to sing to you." He shoved deep.

White clouds streaked the sky. Instead of mountaintops, she saw a cityscape. It felt different, being in Griffin's arms here in Nashville. Not wrong exactly but she still longed for home.

Nola stared out the window, her body still humming from two orgasms. Lyric had finally dropped off to sleep with her bottle, and Griffin had let her lay where she conked out. Then he'd picked Nola up and taken her to bed, where he'd fingered her pussy until she'd stifled another cry of bliss.

The ridge of his cock rode along her thigh, and she wrapped her fingers around his length. The velvety skin against her palm made her mouth water.

She met his intense stare and slid down his body. She breathed in his masculine musk. Leaning close, she nuzzled his erect shaft. He moaned, tangling his fingers in her hair.

"Fuck, I've missed you."

"I've been dreaming about this for months," she said and opened her mouth over the tip of his cock. Her own flavors mingled with his. The instant she sucked him into her throat, shock hit her.

They hadn't used a condom. No protection. Nothing.

She went still. Would it be so bad to have his child? Even though her career was just a fledgling, would it matter? For nine months she could strut around a stage and sing her heart out. Then she'd go home to Reedy and spend a few months on the ranch as a family.

She quit caring about the fact that he'd come inside her and glided her tongue down the underside of his shaft. He tensed. "Gorgeous woman. Suck my cock and then I'll flip you over and lick your—"

She glanced up his body as his words strangled to a stop.

"We didn't use protection," he rasped.

She sucked him back to the tip and dipped her tongue into the depression, collecting the cream. She pulled back. "I know."

"God, I'm sorry. I never thought."

"We'll worry about it later. I wanted you. I'm not stopping now." To her, she meant more than sex. She wanted it all—Griffin, Lyric, his mother. She'd shuttle between Nashville and Reedy, drag them on tours if he was willing. Her income could be put to good use in hiring a ranch hand to keep up the property while they were away.

His eyelids fluttered as she clamped her lips around his cock again and sucked him. The flared head oozed pre-come onto her tongue. She swallowed around him, and he bucked into her mouth.

"Enough. Jeezus. I can't hold off if you do that." He hauled her up his body, and she licked her lips.

Griffin flipped her onto the mattress and plastered his body to hers. Every inch of her felt swollen and ripe, needy. He eased a hand between her thighs and pressed on her aching button. She cried out, and he did a figure eight over her clit, painting her with her wetness.

"Hell, baby doll. You're going to kill me."

"I want to scream your name until everyone in the building knows who I belong to," she said, thinking of the time he'd promised not to stop eating her pussy until everyone in Cheyenne knew his name.

Grinning, he climbed off the bed and disappeared. When he returned he had a condom in hand. She admired his tanned muscles and the long erection jutting from his body. Dark hair sprinkled his arms and legs. Excitement fluttered in her belly. He fisted his cock and pumped it in a smooth stroke. She let her legs fall apart, giving him a view of her wet folds.

"Fucking beautiful," he grated out, rolling the condom in place. He took two steps to the bed and pinned her, drilling her with his gaze. "Wrap those purty little thighs around me." He slapped her outer thigh lightly, and she gasped at the sting.

Damn, she'd missed this. The playful Griffin. And she'd lain in bed many a night, hungering for his demands.

Need coiled in her belly, and she pressed her pussy into him. He captured her lips and drove into her in one solid thrust. She cried out as he stretched her walls. He pinched one nipple between his fingers and rolled it until she thought she'd swoon from the pressure.

She jerked her hips, and he pulled out almost to the tip. She mewled her displeasure, and that bad-boy grin spread over his handsome face.

"Cup your tits together so I can lick them."

Dizziness washed over her at his erotic words. She did as he asked, pressing her breasts tight together. He drove into her body and laved one nipple then the other. Juices spilled over him.

"What I wouldn't give for a toy right now," he murmured against her skin.

She stared at his tongue moving over her nipples. "What?"

"A toy. I'd fuck your pussy and ass at the same time."

She darted a look at her nightstand.

He lifted his head and followed her gaze. Electricity ripped through her body at the look on his face. He rolled off her and lunged for the drawer. When he came up with a slim vibrator and a tube of lube, he looked as if he'd just won a prize.

He ran his tongue over his lower lip. "Ass in the air."

She huffed out a breath. Apprehension mixed with a heady need. He was going to fill her in all ways, control her body as she never had been before.

He was the perfect man for the job.

She flipped onto her stomach.

"Holy fucking hell." The snick of the tube opening awakened every nerve in her body. She held her breath as he smeared the lube over her ass. Goose bumps erupted on her skin. Her nipples ached against the sheets.

"I'm going to ready you for this." He switched on the dildo and the vibrations ran over her skin. He probed her nether hole with a finger. She clamped around his invasion, too well remembering how it felt to have him buried deep inside her.

He worked his finger in and out until she loosened. Then he added a second finger. A pulsation began deep in her core. She focused on the tightening knot.

He smoothed a hand over her ass cheek as he fingered her. "Beautiful skin, such an amazing ass. You want me to slide this into you while I fuck you, don't you?"

"Y-yes." She hitched her hips higher into the air, drawing his two fingers deeper.

"Hell, baby doll. You get me so worked up." He slipped his fingers out, and the vibrator touched her rosette. "Take this, then I'll push my cock into your pussy."

She sucked in a sharp breath as he fitted the vibrator in her ass. When he turned it on again, she cried out. The sensations rocketed her to the peak in seconds. She twisted the sheets in her fists, just as he gathered her hair in his free hand and pulled lightly.

He pumped the probe slowly in and out of her body until she felt on the verge of collapse. Just when she thought she couldn't live through more pleasure, he eased his cock into her.

The fullness stole her sanity. She thrust back, impaling herself on the toy and his shaft. The prickle in her scalp increased. Her breaths came in short pants, fluttering the cotton under her face.

"Fuck, fuck. I can feel those vibrations," he bit off, grinding his cock in her pussy. "Come with me, baby doll. Come now."

He pumped the dildo in time to his thrusts. One plunge...two. On the third, she shattered. Dark pressure burst in a blinding firework. She rode a wave of ecstasy, body thrumming around him. The heat of his release warmed her insides and she fleetingly thought of binding herself to him with a child.

She'd never run as Lyric's mother had. Miranda's loss was Nola's gain.

Satisfaction spread through Nola's body and gripped her heart. Griffin pulled out the vibrator and switched it off. Then he collapsed over her, driving her down into the mattress.

His weight felt like heaven. Their breaths created a new rhythm, and his heart seemed to throb in time to hers. He dropped tiny kisses to her face. When he grew lax and slipped from her body, she missed him. He disappeared into the bathroom and returned without the condom.

He flopped onto the pillow and gathered her against his chest. She tensed as awareness came over her. This was the perfect time for that marriage proposal.

Silence stretched. She heard things she never had before—a dull drone of a ceiling fan, the clatter of garbage cans in the alley below. She swallowed hard and ran a hand down his sculpted chest. His six-pack rippled.

Still, the question didn't come. She pressed her lips together and tried to think of something to fill the quiet.

Why didn't she just ask him to marry her? He'd taken the step more than once, only to be greeted by her bad responses. He was probably afraid of more rejection.

"Come home with me, Nola. Not forever. Just for a little bit."

She pushed out a disappointed breath. Maybe this was all

they'd have—loving ties, weekend visits.

But dammit, she wanted everything—old, new, borrowed, blue boots on her and Lyric, and a promise of a perfectly dirty honeymoon.

He'd changed her, and she was no longer satisfied with only making it in Nashville. She'd come this far in the fairy tale—she was damn well going to get the whole deal.

She leaned onto her elbows and stared at his rugged features. "I'll come next week."

His eyes crinkled with his smile.

She nuzzled his jaw, marking herself with his beard.

"You won't be sorry, baby doll."

# Chapter Seventeen

Griffin glanced at the clock for the tenth time in an hour.

"Her plane's not gonna arrive any sooner because you keep looking at the clock," Taylor drawled.

A smile carved itself around one corner of Griffin's mouth. "Thanks for the reminder. Now, I've got the food." He patted the picnic basket.

"And the champagne?" Taylor cocked a brow.

"'Course. What man proposes without champagne?"

Taylor leaned against the counter and crossed his legs at the ankles. "You're really gonna do this? Tether yourself to one woman?"

Griffin met his gaze. "If she'll have me. She's all I want."

"Well, I'm glad you've found her. Some of us haven't been so lucky. And she's younger." He waggled his brows.

Griffin huffed with laughter. "I'm hoping I can keep up in the years to come."

"That's why they make a blue pill, my friend." Taylor pushed away from the counter and walked across the kitchen to clamp a hand on Griffin's shoulder. "Good luck. You need me to help you load those jars into the truck?"

"Nah, they're in two boxes, all ready to go." Griffin grabbed the basket and followed Taylor out to the truck. Evening was falling, and Nola's late flight would be arriving soon. Griffin had a long drive home from the airport—time to gauge her comfort level with him.

When they were together in Nashville, she'd been sweet and tender with him, doe-eyed and receptive of his kisses, caresses.

She'd sat on the carpet with him and Lyric, playing and talking for three days before he'd taken his leave. She'd seen him off at the airport, a teary-eyed mess.

Those tears gave him hope that she felt as strongly as he did. And that this time when he asked her to marry him, she'd say yes. His plans tonight would hopefully improve his chances of putting a ring on her finger.

Griffin loaded the basket into the truck then saw Taylor off. He watched his friend go, glad Taylor had stuck around through the patches of their friendship Griffin had neglected it. In the past few months he'd concluded that he couldn't take anyone for granted. Soon they wouldn't be there.

In the past he'd driven Nola off with the way he treated her. But never again. If she'd have him, he'd treat her like a queen every day of her life.

He went back to the house for the mason jars. Before he hefted the weight of one box into his arms, he glanced over each jar. A small white candle was situated in each, and a lighter rattled in the bottom of the box. He made two trips to the car. Then he went back inside to find Tessa.

The older woman had Lyric snuggled on her lap, and they were turning the pages of a board book. Lyric's eyes were wide and fixed on the colorful pictures, and Tessa read in a sing-song voice.

She looked up at Taylor's entrance. A smile crossed her face. "You're all set?"

"Yep." He hitched a thumb in the pocket of his jeans. "I'm about to take off."

Her smile broadened. "Good luck to you, young man."

He scuffed a boot along the carpet. "Not sure I'm young any more, but I feel it. She makes me feel it. And she does too." He pointed to Lyric. Then he came forward and dropped a kiss on Lyric's head, resisting the urge to pick her up and cuddle her before he left. If he did, she'd want him to hold her and throw a fit when Tessa took her again.

Lyric's baby smell clung to him as he straightened. "You've got my cell number if anything goes wrong."

Tessa waved a hand. "Go get that young singer and make her yours. Don't worry about Lyric. We'll be waiting to celebrate with you when you come home."

Griffin's chest tightened at what he was about to do. Making a big production of a proposal may not help. She still might turn him down.

"Okay, I'm outta here."

"Luck!" Tessa called to his back. Before he left the house, he heard her resume reading the book to Lyric.

Again he checked that he had everything set for tonight. The truck contained everything he needed from condoms to a good bottle of champagne. He thought about getting a backup lighter for the candles, then resisted.

"Just get on with it," he muttered and climbed into the truck.

He bounced across the field to the perfect location. The grass was shorter after a first cutting for hay, and the blades would cradle the mason jars so they didn't fall over. The land sloped gently upward, so his message would be easily read.

He spent half an hour setting up the jars in a certain order. When the candles were lit, they'd spell *Marry Me*. He'd keep Nola in the truck some distance away while he lit the candles, then bring her down here.

Satisfied with the results, he hopped back into the truck and headed to the airport. During the long drive, his mind never quit. He raced over several scenarios.

Nola leaping into his arms, wrapping her legs around his waist and kissing him between whispers of "yes".

Or pushing her red-gold hair off her face and turning a distressed gaze upon him. Trying to let him down gently, explaining she had a new career ahead of her and she didn't want to be tied to an older cowboy with a daughter and a town she'd just escaped.

He pressed his lips into a line and watched a jet soar low, angling for the runway. Her plane landed in twenty minutes—just enough time for him to park and freak himself out waiting.

Before he went into the terminal, he grabbed a bouquet of wildflowers he'd stopped to pick on the way out of Reedy. The late blooms were everywhere right now. He'd considered a store-bought bouquet, but this fit him better.

He prayed they fit Nola too.

After finding her gate, he paced. The airport was quieter at this time of night. The sun had long ago faded from the sky, dropping out of sight as he reached his destination.

By the time they got back home and to the field where he planned his surprise, it would be the wee hours of the night. Somehow that made it seem more romantic.

People began to file out of the gate, and he tensed, waiting to catch a glimpse of the red-gold head he loved. His heart thrummed.

When she appeared, she immediately began searching the area for him, straining onto tiptoes to see over the people.

A thousand butterflies hatched in his stomach as he surged forward. She saw him and bounced into the air. Twice.

His heart soared. "Nola," he grated out as he pushed past a woman and caught Nola in his arms.

She glued herself to him, arms around his neck, body flush against his. Arousal tore through him, and his cock jerked at her nearness. Heat clawed at his insides as he drew in a deep gulp of her scent.

She tipped up her face and their gazes locked for a strong heartbeat before he crushed his mouth to hers. She made a soft noise in her throat and wound herself more tightly around him.

He pulled her out of the way, still kissing her, the bouquet squashed against her spine. A few stems broke, and flowers skimmed his knuckles, but he didn't care. She was here with him, in his arms. And he wasn't letting her go.

He drew back to look at her. It didn't matter she was wearing designer clothes and a glittering necklace, because her smile was all he cared about. Her full lips stretched over her white teeth, and his cock surged again at the thought of the blowjob she'd blown his mind with before he left Nashville.

Her eyes grew hooded. Could she be thinking that too?

"I'm sorry for treating you like I did, baby doll."

She shook her head. "I can see by the look on your face you won't do it again. I have some things to be sorry for too. When you called, I couldn't bring myself to speak to you. Not after what I'd done with your song." She dropped her gaze. "I'm sorry."

He used a knuckle to lift her chin. Their gazes met, and everything was healed.

She ran a hand down his shirt front. "You look gorgeous. Like home."

His throat clogged at her words, and he pulled the flowers around her body and placed them under her nose.

"Thank you," she said thickly, burying her nose in the blooms. The pink petals kissed her skin, casting a rosier glow.

"How much luggage do you have?" He removed the long strap of a carry-on bag from her shoulder and wound an arm around her waist.

"This is it. If I need more clothes, there are some at my parents'." She pointed to the carry-on and stared at his lips.

"What's wrong?"

"Are you gonna kiss me again or not?" Her voice came out soft, but every cell in his body heard her and responded.

"Hell yeah, baby doll." He enfolded her in his arms again

215

and plunged his tongue between her lips. That she longed for more ignited him fully. His cock throbbed against his fly, demanding exit. He angled his head and swept her mouth with his tongue.

Her round breasts pressed against his chest, and he lifted a hand. Then remembering where they were, he dropped it to her waist. Gripping her hard, he probed the hollow above her hipbone with his thumb until she squirmed.

She tore away, breathless. "Let's..."

"Get goin'." He gripped her hand and led her out of the airport. He stuffed her into the truck with all haste, wanting to lock her away and never let her escape.

But she still might. He sucked in a deep breath and walked around to the driver's door. When he climbed in, he found her nose in the wildflower bouquet again.

"These are my favorites. Did you know?" Her voice was still thick, her eyes shining in the dim lighting from the parking lamps.

He twisted the key in the ignition. "I do now."

During the drive back to the ranch, she locked their fingers together and talked about Nashville. Things were happening fast for her, and her song—their song—was still riding high in the charts. She had performances booked on nighttime entertainment TV shows, and they were about to record her whole album.

"So you've been writing?" he asked, glancing at her profile, striking in the moonlight.

She looked at him again, her eyes softer yet. "You can't imagine how much I wrote after you left me a week ago."

He didn't ask for more. It was enough.

By the time they trundled up the driveway, Nola had curled against his side, her head on his shoulder. When he rolled past the house and out through the field, she sat up straighter.

"Where are we going?"

He dropped a kiss to her temple, nuzzling her fragrant skin. "You'll see."

They bounced across the field, but he stopped some distance away from the place he'd set up the jars. She pivoted on the seat, bringing her denim-clad knees close to his. He stroked her silky fingers, and she looked at him expectantly.

Moonlight fell over her. It only enhanced her beauty.

"Give me five minutes. Stay here." His voice sounded rough.

She nodded.

He got out of the truck, his heart racing. But he loped around a row of trees and across the field to the mason jars. As he lit the candles in each, his mind rushed ahead. To their wedding day and how good she'd be for Lyric.

When he had the candles all lit, he stood back and looked at the effect. The countryside glowed. Nola would look gorgeous amidst the candlelight, out here under the big Wyoming sky where she belonged.

He pocketed the lighter and practically ran back to the truck. Nola waited for him, twisting her hands in her lap. He unclenched her fingers and tugged her out into his arms. She clung to him for a long moment, and he couldn't resist brushing his lips over hers.

The kiss quickly heated, but he pulled away. "Come with me." On the way past the truck bed, he grabbed the basket and hooked it over his arm.

She grinned, eyes twinkling. Though she seemed happy, he worried. Overall she was quiet tonight.

As they neared the place he planned to propose, he had eyes only for her. When the candle glow kissed her skin, he watched her face. Her long brows knit in the middle. She shook her head, sending waves of hair bouncing over her breasts.

His heart plummeted. She was going to say no. It was over.

He'd lost her.

Her mouth opened then closed.

He pushed out the breath he was holding. "Well?"

"I don't... ARR?"

Confusion shot through his brain. He jerked around to look at the field. Half of the candles had blown out, leaving only ARR.

He dropped to his knees before her, gathering her hands in his. "Marry me. It's supposed to be *Marry Me*. Marry me, Nola."

She held his gaze for a long moment then threw her head back and released a laugh to the sky. When she looked at him again, he didn't know whether to laugh with her or cry.

She skimmed her fingers over his jaw. "I thought you'd turned pirate on me for a moment."

His chest convulsed with laughter that was almost a sob. He pressed his face to her belly, so terrified of never having her as his wife. "Well?" he asked against her shirt.

She shifted against him, falling to her knees. She cupped his face and stared deep into his eyes. "A thousand times yes, Griffin."

His heart flipped and excitement doused the fear. He'd jumped again and landed safely on the other side. "Really?"

"I'd hoped you'd ask in Nashville. I would have said yes then."

So disappointment had crept in. He wrapped his arms around her and threw them backward. They rolled in the grass, her body plastered to him.

"My wife. You'll be my wife!" He wanted to roar it to the pinpricks of light shining down on them.

She raised herself over him, her eyes glazed with passion. "I can't imagine not having you in my life forever, Griffin. And Lyric. I want Lyric as my daughter."

Tears burned his nose. "She's yours already, baby doll. And

218

me...I've been yours since the moment I saw you in The Hellion. Nashville can have you when necessary, but I want you on my ranch. In my bed."

She shivered, and he smoothed his hands down her bare arms. Her skin was cool, but not for long. He planned to heat every inch with his kisses.

"Reach into that basket. I have a blanket."

She arched a brow. "Spent some time on this event, didn't you?" She tipped to the side and snagged the basket handle. She dragged it across the ground.

"I had to make it perfect so you'd say yes. I couldn't ask one more time." He found the blanket and shook it out. After wrapping it around her, he rolled her so the blanket kept her body from the dew-covered grass and he hovered over her.

Her eyes glowed, reflecting the remaining candle flames. "I wish I would have seen the entire message before it blew out."

"I'll light it for you every year on this date, baby doll. You'll see it fifty more times."


A sound like a sob broke from her. He captured it with his mouth, snaking his tongue between her lips to taste her salty tears. He entangled his fingers in her hair and plied her with kisses so long and deep, her pussy clenched.

Nola's heart was bursting with love and passion for Griffin. At the airport, she'd expected a ring and had been disappointed. When he'd stopped the truck, she'd waited expectantly, but he'd only gotten out.

But when he'd actually said the words, her heart had expanded ten times the size with all the love she felt for him.

She raked her fingers over the hard planes of his back, feeling every ridge and muscle. His harsh breathing matched hers. Something told her this night under the stars would be explosive.

Heat knotted her belly, and she shifted against him, seeking ease from the agony of want.

He ripped his mouth from hers and trailed a path of kisses down her throat to the swells of her breasts. Her nipples puckered, aching for more. He groaned as she arched under him.

"Gorgeous woman. Mine." He found the hem of her shirt and eased his hand under, tunneling right to her aching breast. He squeezed it and she moaned. He turned his face aside, and she surged upward to clamp her lips over the skin of his neck.

She sucked, and he rocked the ridge of his erection into her. When she pulled back, she knew a dark mark would have risen on his skin. "There. You wear the hickeys."

"Gladly." He tugged her shirt up and off, abandoning it in the grass. She gasped at the cool night air kissing her heated flesh. With swift movements, he removed her bra. Before she could shiver from the cold on her breasts, he covered one with a broad palm and took the other in his mouth.

The revolution of his tongue around the hard tip made her cry out. He scraped his teeth gently over it, and juices flooded her pussy.

"Get out of these clothes so I can feel my fiancé's muscles." She plucked at the waist of his jeans, eager to feel his thick length in her hand, her body.

His teeth flashed white as he stripped his shirt off. His carved chest and abs tormented her. Was it possible he looked broader, the cuts of muscle made deeper by shadow? Her mouth watered.

"Keep looking at me like that and I'll never last, woman."

A smile spread over her face and coated her heart too. "Your woman."

"For-fucking-ever." He slammed his mouth over hers, licking, tasting, lapping at her until she thought she'd die from the pressure building in her core.

Dark need made her wrap her legs around his waist. She brought her pussy against his cock. The barrier of their jeans was too much for both of them. He rolled off and fought the denim off his hips, then hers. When they lay bare under the open sky, he covered her with his body once again.

"I have a whole basket full of condoms." He nipped at her breast, plucking the bud with his teeth.

She gasped and encircled the base of his cock with her fingers. He growled. "What else is in that basket?"

"Fruit, champagne. Chocolate."

Her smile widened. "You were really prepared to woo me."

His dark eyes burned into her. "It's going to be our breakfast." With that, he rocked his cock between her thighs, skimming her wet folds. His velvety length was blissful torture. She shifted restlessly, trying to angle him perfectly to slide in. But he resisted.

"Get one of those condoms out, baby doll. I have something to take care of." He slid down her body. When he pressed her legs apart and fanned her soaking pussy with his breath, she quivered with need.

For the past week she'd fantasized about his mouth, lips, tongue on her sensitive nub. He dragged his tongue from bottom to top through her slick folds. When he reached her clit, he opened his mouth and applied pressure to it.

She bucked. He pinned her to the blanket and lashed her straining nubbin with his tongue. Her pussy contracted, and more cream oozed out. She tangled her fingers in the hair on his nape and guided him.

Pressure built. Over the length of her body, his dark eyes glimmered. She watched his tongue circle her clit. Each rotation sent her sailing higher. Her inner thigh muscles shook.

He reached up her body and closed his rough fingers over

each nipple. Twisting them perfectly, he licked her hard nubbin. She stared at the sky. The stars blurred in her vision. Her rasping breaths grew louder until she was screaming with each blissful stroke of his tongue.

Being out here alone, they were more uninhibited than ever. And knowing they'd come back here each year only made her heart fuller.

He pinched her nipples hard. Her body throbbed. Peaked. Waves crashed over her. Her pussy pulsated under his mouth as he drove her on with his sweet torment.

She rocked against him. He released one nipple and thrust two fingers deep in her channel, extending her orgasm. When he curled his fingers against her G-spot, she nearly rocketed upward again.

He lifted his head and gave her nipple one last strum. But he kept his fingers buried in her sheath. "Fucking hell. Damn."

His curses were the best love words she could ask for.

"Your turn," she whispered, grabbing his shoulders.

When she pulled him up the length of her body, he removed his fingers. She moaned at the loss, but planned to regain it. Right after she tasted him too.

She tore open the condom packet and kept the rubber ring in her palm. She made Griffin lie on his back so he could look at the stars while she blew his mind.

She moved down his body, kissing and licking the ridges of his abs. As he realized her goal, he wrapped her hair around his fist. "I can't, baby doll. I'll never hold off."

"I won't let you go that far. I just want a taste." She licked her lips slowly, and a muscle jumped in the crease of his jaw.

He released her hair but kept his warm fingers on her scalp as she opened her mouth over his erection. The mushroom-shaped head filled up her mouth, and she pushed down on it, taking him right to the root.

"Goddamn fuck." His abs flexed as he obviously tried to refrain from pounding into her mouth. "Jesus, you're beautiful. All mine."

She slid her tongue up and down his shaft, riding a thick vein on the side. She reached the tip and lapped it, letting pre-come string between her tongue and his body.

He squeezed his eyes shut. "I can't take any more."

She released his cock and eased the condom over his length. Then she stroked him slowly, rolling the head through her fingers and cupping his balls in her other hand.

"Get up here." His command made her smile.

"Wait. I just want to—" She dipped her head and opened her mouth over his balls, sucking his sac gently.

"Motherfuck. Nola."

She raised her head and ran her tongue over her lips, flavored like him. He issued a growl and yanked her up his body. He positioned her right over his cock and pushed her down with one slick motion.

She moaned as her walls stretched around him. Liquid heat pooled around him. The spot he'd stroked with his fingers throbbed.

"Ride me."

"I'm a cowgirl at heart." She rode his length upward then sank over him once more. He gripped her ass and drove her down farther, grinding his hips and cock into her core. She threw her head back and lost herself to the sensation.

Flames of want licked at her insides as he plunged deep, withdrew, then went deeper yet. She clenched her pussy muscles, milking his every inch.

"How can I hold off when you do that to me?" he rasped.

"Don't. I'm almost there."

His eyes darkened. She wanted to see that expression in them every day of her life—his love and bald desire.

She pressed her palms against his chest, rising and falling on him. A burst of sudden heat stole her breath.

"That's it, baby doll. Come for me." He ground his hips again. His cock passed over the exquisite pressure point.

She fell forward as ecstasy threatened to tear her in half. When he stroked her clit with his thumb, she lost control.

Pleasure curled and broke in her. She met his gaze, tumbling in the dark waters of his love. Juices soaked him. He stiffened, his movements more erratic. Then extreme bliss passed over his rugged features, and he came with a shout.

Liquid warmth filled her. She continued to move over him, stroking long, primal moans from him. Satisfaction spread through her chest.

He slid his arms around her and pulled her so she lay atop him. She went boneless in his hold. Her stuttering breaths slowed. He traced a path down her spine then back up. Each languid pass made her sleepier. She couldn't wait to watch the sun come up with him. And to eat that decadent breakfast.

She smiled against his skin.

A whoosh sounded, and light flared. They jerked and looked up in time to see a ball of flame around one of the Mason jar candles. White light imprinted itself on her retinas, and she blinked.

"What is that?" she asked.

His voice sounded odd. "I think it's your shirt."

Hysterical laughter claimed her as she watched her designer top go up in flames. When he'd thrown it, he'd obviously sent it arcing too close to the jar. Griffin shook under her with his own laughter.

"I always knew you wanted to keep me naked on your ranch, but this is ridiculous." She giggled.

He sobered, staring up at her. Light from her inflamed shirt danced in his eyes.

He lifted her chin. "That song was meant to be sung by you." His words were a rough caress that raised the hair on her body. He enveloped her in his arms again, and they lay together until the candles extinguished and her shirt turned to ash. Only happiness remained.

# Epilogue

A collective "awwwwwww" echoed through the small Reedy church as Lyric toddled down the aisle. Her puffy white dress churned around her chubby legs, and a few flowers were crushed in her fist.

Nola sucked in a deep breath, focusing on the little blue cowgirl boots Lyric wore treading away from her. This was it. Somehow they'd managed to keep the wedding private, admitting only one trusty Reedy photographer who would capture her and Griffin's love. Later he'd sell the pictures to the press. But at least Nola had achieved her goal of not having a bodyguard walk her down the aisle.

Her father beamed at her. His sharp tuxedo fit him impeccably, but the pride in his eyes made him truly handsome. He offered his arm. "Ready, Nola?"

She nodded, her throat suddenly clogged off. She gripped the full skirt of her gown, revealing the toes of her blue boots, and pivoted to face the congregation. Ahead of her Molly practically sashayed down the aisle in a lush satin gown of ice blue. The crowd was on their feet.

Nola's heart fluttered as she raised her gaze, seeking the one person who lit her universe. The notes to "One Lyric" erupted from the organ. It had taken old Mrs. McAllen two full weeks of practice to learn the song, but Nola was thrilled with the outcome.

A smile so wide it made her cheeks ache claimed her face as she set eyes on Griffin. He beamed from the altar, flanked by Taylor and holding Lyric in one arm. The baby fussed with his bowtie, but he didn't remove his gaze from Nola.

As she drifted up the aisle, past the people who had watched her grow up—helped her grow up—and put her hand into Griffin's, she'd never known such elation. At one time she'd thought she couldn't be happy with anything but her dream of becoming a country music singer.

But somehow Molly's notions of being a good wife, of standing by her man, had rubbed off on Nola. Or maybe she'd always possessed these dreams. Either way, she realized she could have both dreams.

"You look beautiful," Griffin rumbled into her ear.

She trailed a finger over the rough, dark hair on his jaw. "You're the fairy tale."

# About the Author

Em Petrova lives in backwoods Pennsylvania, where she raises four kids and a Labradoodle puppy named Daisy Hasselhoff and pays too damn much for utilities. She loves to write gritty characters with lots of heart and is well-known for scorching, panty-soaking erotic romance.

You can find her at http://empetrova.com or holding parties here on Facebook: https://facebook.com/em.petrova.

*It'll take more than rope to tie down the man they love.*

# Unbroken
## © *2013 Em Petrova*
### *Country Fever*, Book 3

When Christian comes out of the bar to find a bat-wielding country girl beating the hell out of his best friend Tucker's truck, he does the only thing he can—he flirts with her. Unfortunately, he knows her pain—he's in love with Tucker too.

Claire plans to nurse her bruised heart alone, but inevitably Tucker draws her back in—along with Christian—and the three of them tumble headlong into delirious passion. Then she and Christian wake to find that Tucker has fled his horse ranch, leaving them to care for the animals and each other.

Still grieving the death of his fiancée, pressured to sign over mining rights to a coal company, Tucker is boots-deep in emotional turmoil. Running only sharpens his longing for what he truly wants—Christian and Claire in his bed, in the barn, and under the stars.

But roping themselves firmly inside the circle of love will take everything they have—bulldogged determination, flying fists and aching hearts.

*Warning: Wrangle one heartsick cowboy, and the man and woman who love him. Throw in weeks of working in close quarters, bales of pent-up lust, and feel the burn of prairie-fire-hot desire. Now just try to walk away with your heart unbranded.*

*Available now in ebook and print from Samhain Publishing.*

*Sometimes, a girl has to take more than one bull by the horns.*

# Boots and Buckles
## © *2013 Myla Jackson*
### *Ugly Stick Saloon*, Book 6

Mona Daley has had her fill of rodeo cowboys. Especially after Grant Raleigh and his partner blew through town three years ago. A torrid affair, a promise to return, then...nothing.

Chalking it up to girl-in-every-town syndrome, she swore off buckle-bearing cowpokes and never looked back. Now she's working nights at the Ugly Stick Saloon to make enough money to save her beauty salon.

Grant has plans for his return to Mona's life, plans that include groveling at her feet for another chance. Except his roping partner, Sam Whitefeather, gets to her first—and it looks like they've hit it off.

If he thought Mona didn't harbor feelings for him, Grant would be the decent guy, step aside, and let her be happy. But one look, one touch on the dance floor and he finds himself falling all over again. He's determined to prove his sincerity and that he's the better man for her. Even if it means squaring off in the hottest arena imaginable—the bedroom.

*Warning: The rodeo's coming to town and there's nothing two hot cowboys can't do with a rope, a willing woman, and a lot of imagination.*

*Available now in ebook from Samhain Publishing.*

SAMHAIN
PUBLISHING

*It's all about the story...*

# Romance

# HORROR

www.samhainpublishing.com

CPSIA information can be obtained at www.ICGtesting.com
Printed in the USA
LVOW11s0623290815

452043LV00002B/262/P